The Village Indian

THE
SEAGULL
LIBRARY OF
GERMAN
LITERATURE

The Village Indian

ABBAS KHIDER

Translated by Donal McLaughlin

LONDON NEW YORK CALCUTTA

This publication was supported by a grant from the Goethe-Institut India

Seagull Books, 2019

First published in German as *Der falsche Inder* by Abbas Khider

First published in English translation by Seagull Books, 2013

ISBN 978 0 8574 2 101 2

British Library Cataloguing-in-Publication Data
A catalogue record for this book is available from the British Library.

Typeset by Seagull Books, Calcutta, India
Printed and bound by WordsWorth India, New Delhi, India

For those who, a second before they die,
still dream of two wings

'The Intercity-Express 1511 from Berlin to Munich, calling at Leipzig, Bamberg, Nuremberg and Ingolstadt, will depart from Platform 3 at 12.57.' The voice over the speaker: unpleasantly tinny. A brief glance at the large clock on the platform: 12.30. Just under half an hour to go. I put my paper and coffee down on the bench. Zoo Station. I cast my eye over it again.

Empty. Totally empty. The feeling, for a moment, that I'm all alone on the platform. That the people have vanished or that perhaps were never there at all. Empty. And all bright and clean. No trains, no passengers, no announcements. Nothing—only me and an empty Zoo Station, the vast nothingness round me. Where am I? What am I doing here? Where's everyone else? Questions like these boom in my head—like drums at an African festival. Empty, like a never-ending desert, bare mountains or clear water. Eerie too, like a forest after a violent storm. And my questions, loud, yet quiet; echoing, though unvoiced.

This feeling lasts for a few minutes—or is it more than that? It's not the first time I've felt so disoriented. It's been like this for a few years now. I worry, sometimes, that there'll come a day when I won't find my way back out. Of this madness. This desert in my head.

The station concourse, thank God, is still there. The graffiti on the walls too. 'My joker's no longer a joke.' 'Simone is my babe.' The curried-sausage and hotdog stands . . . The people . . .

12.40. I cast my eye over the station again. This time there are no African drums. The platform, full. Passengers boarding trains or looking for an exit. Some running, so as not to miss connections. A group of half-naked girls and boys, in short trousers and summer tops, stroll along the platform, carrying their rucksacks. Like a bunch of schoolchildren, almost. The girls are laughing, their loud, clear voices bring the station to life. A few older people ahead of them. Their teachers, perhaps—their faces serious. Almost all of them are pulling a black case.

Pigeons, wherever you look. They've even made nests under the roof. A male bird is seducing a female. The male spreads his feathers, drags them along behind him, then swaggers round the female, flirting. 'Coo, coo. Coo, coo.' The female, head held high, struts up and down before him like a queen. She moves, at times slowly, at times quickly, driving him wild. Not far from them, a schoolboy is chatting up a girl, or trying to. The girl smiles. Bravely, he swaggers round her. She takes off for the exit and he follows, blindly. 'Lukas, come back,' one of the male teachers shouts after him.

12.45. The train approaches. I find my reserved seat in the smoking compartment. Put the rucksack between my feet. Place a notebook, a book, a packet of cigarettes and a lighter on the table. Light a cigarette . . .

13.02. A little late, the train begins to move. On the seat next to me I spot a big, fat envelope. A whole wad of papers in it, it seems. On the outside, in squiggly writing, the Arabic word for 'memories'. The person next to me has gone to the toilet, perhaps. Or to the restaurant car. He'll be back soon, for sure. I'm already looking forward to speaking Arabic, to the opportunity. With a poet perhaps. Someone interested in words, at least. In reading and writing.

13.30. My neighbour still hasn't come back. He'll be back soon. Won't leave the envelope lying here for ever. Where might he be from? There are so many Arab states. I hope he's from one I know well. If so, we'll have plenty to chat about.

14.16. The train is almost at the next stop. 'Next stop, Leipzig,' the voice drones from the speaker. The envelope is still here. A few people get off, a few get on. A girl sits opposite me. Headphones on, she's listening to music on her MP3 player. A boy sits in the seat beside her and turns on his laptop. A lady with short, blond hair and talking on her mobile phone, tries to sit next to me. She gives me an annoyed look, reaches for the envelope, drops it on my lap, occupies the seat and—cool as you please—continues with her call.

What was that all about? Who does she think she is? Such inconsiderate behaviour! Should I tell her the envelope isn't mine? God! She's still on the phone! About fifty, probably. Looks like a lot of women do in this country—bit of lipstick, skirt, blouse, a mini-handbag that'd suit a queen bee better, black high heels. They're unpredictable, women like that. Best stay calm . . .

14.20. The train moves off, slowly. I lift the envelope carefully, leave the compartment and go in search of the restaurant. The pretty young waitress brings me a large coffee really quickly. In front of me, on the small table, the envelope. A difficult decision. Should I give it to the conductor? Explain it's lost property? My curiosity is too great, though. I decide to open it and read what's inside, before—perhaps—handing it in.

Outside the window, the bottle-green landscape is glowing in the sun. I sip my coffee. Light a cigarette. Eye the waitress. She's young. Eighteen to twenty, say. Her hair's dyed red and she's wearing the familiar blue jacket of the Deutsche Bahn, but with jeans and a white T-shirt, 'Sexy Girl' printed on it. Small, firm breasts support the lettering.

I take my coffee and the envelope and return to my seat in the compartment. The lady is still on the phone, the boy is still hammering on his laptop and the girl is still enjoying her music.

14.45. The train moves on.

I open the envelope.

Memories

RASUL HAMID

There are two things: emptiness
and the I portrayed.

Gottfried Benn

ONE

The Village Indian

WHEN, IN 762, Caliph al-Mansur was travelling through the vast expanses of the Orient in search of rest and calm, his eyes suddenly fell on an idyllic landscape between two rivers. Without a moment's thought, he ordered his soldiers to dig a large ditch round this piece of land, fill it with wood and light a fire at dusk. As the flames flared, he looked down from a nearby hill and announced, 'Here is where my city shall be founded.' And he named the city Madinat al-Salam, the city of peace, known today as Baghdad. The city of peace has never known peace. And again and again, rulers have stood on the hill and watched it burn.

I was born in this fire, in this city, perhaps that's why my skin is this coffee colour. I was well grilled—like mutton—over the fire. For me, the ghosts of the fire have always been present, I've seen the city burn time and again. One war embraced another. One catastrophe followed the next. Each time, Baghdad, or all of Iraq—in the skies and on the ground—burnt: from 1980 to 1988 in the First Gulf War; from 1988 to 1989 in the war that the Ba'ath regime waged against the Iraqi Kurds; in the Second Gulf War in 1991; in the same year again, during the Iraqi uprising; in 2003, in the Third Gulf War; and, in between, in hundreds of smaller fires, battles, uprisings and skirmishes. Fire is this country's fate, and even the waters of the two great rivers, the Euphrates and the Tigris, are powerless against it.

Even the sun in Baghdad is friends with the fire ghosts. In summer, it never wants to go down and rolls through the city, like a carriage of iron and fire, slashing the horizon's face, shunting its aimless way through the streets and houses. Is this merciless sun the reason for my burnt and dusty looks? Yet, my birthday is on 3 March, long before the hot season with its temperatures of up to fifty degrees. Or is the heat of the oven to blame for my dark skin? If—as she always said—I really did drop from my mother's belly in the kitchen, then I must have spent many hours there, even as a newborn, right next to the stove where black beans and aubergine were often cooking. I suspect that the stone oven on which my mother baked our bread did its bit too. How I loved to watch as my mother took the pitta, when it was ready, from the oven and threw them onto a large palm-leaf plate at her feet. Each and every time, I'd sneak up to the hot bread. Each and every time, I'd feel the irresistible urge to touch it, only to burst out crying when I'd again burn my fingers. And each and every time, I'd remain sitting as close as I could to that fascinating stone-oven fire.

So, I have several possible explanations for my dark skin: the rulers' fire and the Baghdad sun, the heat of the kitchen and the stone-oven embers. They're all responsible for the fact that I go through life with brown skin, the darkest black hair and dark eyes.

But if these factors made me the way I am, why don't the other inhabitants of this two-river country look the same? Some do, but I remain so different that people tend to doubt my Iraqi origins. Often, in Baghdad, the bus conductors addressed me in English. I'd just laugh, answer in the vernacular of southern Iraq and leave them staring at me, baffled, as if they'd seen a ghost. The same thing would happen, occasionally, at police checks, and I'd have to answer long lists of questions: What do Iraqis like to eat? What songs are sung to Iraqi children? Which are the best-known Iraqi tribes? Only when I'd answered them all correctly and my Iraqi origins had been proven beyond doubt was I permitted to carry on. The boys in my part of town called me 'The Red Indian' because I looked like the Indians in American cowboy films. At intermediate school, they called me 'Indian' or 'Amitabh Bachchan', after a famous Indian actor I really did look a little like, a tall, thin, brown fellow.

My father was the only person who had a totally different explanation, something really exciting. He took me aside one day—I must have been about fifteen. 'Son,' he said, 'your real mother's a gypsy. That's why you don't look like your brothers!' He kept it short. They'd had an affair. She was called Selwa. 'One of the most beautiful women in the world, she was,' he claimed proudly. 'Had a butterfly ever landed on her, her beauty would have made it wilt.'

The story began in Baghdad, in al-Kamaliya, a part of town close to ours. A dancer, she was, and a woman of the night. My father was her best customer. She loved him and wanted a child by him and then had that child. My father, though, didn't want a gypsy to be the mother of one of his children. So, with the men of our tribe, he decided to drive her and her family out of the district but only after taking the baby from her. No sooner said than done. I was accepted into the tribe and the gypsies were chased away. Later, it was rumoured that Selwa had moved with her people to northern Iraq, then left them to migrate alone to Turkey and then to Greece. She'd worked there for a while, for an Egyptian in a dance club, but then killed herself. My stepmother never spoke about it. She brought me up as if I were her own.

The funny thing about this story is that both my mothers have the same name: Selwa. My non-gypsy mother claimed that my father was a liar and I her flesh and blood. Once, she even brought home an old lady who insisted she was present at my birth. She swore on all the prophets that my non-gypsy mother Selwa had indeed given birth to me in the kitchen. The gypsy story I only heard from my father. Once, I even went to al-Kamaliya, aka 'Whore and Pimp District', where there really was no shortage of brothels. I asked if they knew a gypsy called Selwa and her people. No one did though. That's why I doubt there's anything at all to that story. My father only told it to me, I suppose, to punish me—because I couldn't stand him.

I didn't see the story as a punishment at all. Why should I? What was wrong with gypsies? Beautiful women full of fire and passion, whom every man desired. When I was a child, boys used to fight for a chance to watch when, in their skimpy, colourful skirts, the women danced, half naked, at weddings and other parties. I remember how the men's hungry eyes devoured them. The male gypsies, too, were so handsome that the men in our part of town thought they had to lock their doors to keep their women safe. Always, I believe, when the gypsies had been at one of our weddings, the women round us revelled for weeks in the memory—their black hair, their deep, big bull eyes, their firm muscles and brown bodies, glistening with sweat beneath the blazing lights of the wedding party—and wished they could feel them beneath the covers at night as their hands tried to satiate their unfulfilled desires. It'd hardly have been any different for the men, thinking of those gypsy women, so full of fire.

I really was one of the best-looking boys in our part of town. It's possible I inherited my looks from my gypsy mother: the colour of my skin, my long, dark curly hair and my big, black, gentle eyes. I adored the gypsies, after all, and the songs they sang. For a long time I carried about a picture of a dancing gypsy woman in my trouser pocket. Nonetheless, I decided to accept my non-gypsy mother as my 'proper mother'. She was my guardian angel and she loved me more than all my brothers and sisters, her biological children.

The question of whether gypsies are really from India, as some scientists claim, has always interested me. I hope, secretly, the theory is true. I could then initiate myself as an Indian Iraqi gypsy and put an end to all my existential questions! If not, then there must be some other concrete link between me and India, for that country has always haunted me, always played a role in my life.

When, after the Second Gulf War in March 1991, the Shi'ites revolted against the regime, the Iraqi government claimed in its press that these were not real Iraqis but Indian immigrants whose ancestors had come to Iraq in the eighteenth century. The problem was that the theory was rejected by all notable historians as there seemed to be no scientific proof whatsoever for it. But then, they didn't know me either—living proof that the Shi'ites perhaps *could* have come from India.

IN THE FIRST YEARS OF THE THIRD DECADE OF MY LIFE, I fled from the endless fire of the rulers and the merciless Baghdad sun. My path took me through various countries. I lived for a while in Africa, in Libya, with the result that words from the Libyan vernacular began to mix with my Iraqi ones. That led to my next problem. I spent a while in Tripoli, where I met a few Iraqis in a cafe on the beach. When I introduced myself, they responded angrily, 'Do you think we're stupid? You're not Iraqi! You don't look Iraqi, and the way you speak isn't right either!' When I later went to Tunisia, it was very different. In the capital, I noticed right away that the women were round me like bees round honey. In the centre, on Avenue Bourguiba, a group of girls followed me with their flirtatious eyes, shouting to each other quite openly, 'Hey, check out the good-looking Indian!' For a whole month I had great fun with the most beautiful women in the streets of Tunis, pretending to be an Indian tourist looking for a guide. And that's how I found a short-lived love: Iman. For her, my hair was the eighth wonder of the world.

In Africa, no one had a problem with my appearance. I wasn't blond, and the children didn't crowd round me, clapping, like they did round the Europeans. The colour of my skin was an advantage. Compared with the locals, I was even regarded by some as white. Everything else, though—life itself, every aspect of it—was in no way easy there, which is why I planned to head to Europe. But the journey was only possible along illegal routes.

IN EUROPE, my appearance again attracted trouble. It started in Athens. In the beginning, fortunately, I had no big problems and I didn't have to worry about being arrested. There were so many refugees in the country that they'd have needed millions of prisons to lock them all up. From time to time, nonetheless, the police arrested a few—probably to make it *look* like they were doing something about the refugee problem. Once, they caught me too. I spent a few days in a cell while they tried to arrange a refugee ID card for me.

On the final day, something tragic happened. I needed to go to the toilet. A policeman accompanied me. On the way back he blocked my path and, in a fit of rage, began to beat me. I didn't understand what was happening and began to shout as loudly as I could. Some of the other policemen came running and saved me from the blows of my escort who seemed to have gone mad. They began to grumble and argue with him. Such a commotion! I didn't understand a word but guessed that they were angry with him for attacking me. Suddenly, the raging policeman was cowering on the floor, hitting himself in the face and howling. How absurd! I couldn't make any sense of it! A blond policeman brought me back to my cell. I sat there, fed up with the world, hugely disappointed and sad. I couldn't believe that in Europe too the police kicked and beat people for no reason. I could never have imagined it. A horrible surprise! In the evening, the door opened and an officer in a smart uniform entered my cell. He had an array of stars and other insignias all over his chest and shoulders. He explained in English that the policeman had lost his head because he thought I was a Pakistani drug dealer the Greek police had been after for a long time. He had, it seemed, lost his youngest brother to an overdose. And because he thought I was that drug dealer, his rage had boiled over and he had lost all self-control. The officer showed me a photo of the dealer. It was hard to believe—he really did look just like me! Two peas in a pod, we seemed to be. I was confused, myself.

Half an hour later, the no-longer-raging policeman returned and pointed his finger at me. 'Are you from Iraq?' he asked in English.

'Yes!'

'Sorry!'

He closed the door and left. Fifteen minutes later, a different policeman came, gave me an ID, accompanied me to the front door and said, again in English, 'Go!'

I LEFT GREECE AND ITS POLICE and fled to Germany. In Germany, things were the same and yet they were different. The overzealousness of the German police brought my illegal journey to an abrupt end—in the middle of Bavaria. I wanted, actually, to continue to Sweden for I'd heard from lots of other refugees that you got support from the state to learn Swedish and study at university. Nothing like that existed in Germany, apparently. I was on the train from Munich to Hamburg and from there, via Denmark, to Sweden. When it stopped at the station of a small town called Ansbach, two Bavarian policemen came on board. They didn't ask any of the many blond passengers for their ID but came straight to me. Was it my Indian looks?

'Passport?'

'No!'

They arrested me. At the police station, my appearance caused further excitement. The officers simply wouldn't believe I was Iraqi—they thought I was an Indian or a Pakistani claiming to be Iraqi to get asylum. A fraud, in other words. Given the dictatorship in our country, Iraqis, at the time, were eligible for asylum in Germany, unlike the citizens of many other countries, Indians and Pakistanis, for example. It took a long time for an interpreter and a judge from Nuremberg to arrive in order to test me with a whole set of questions. They wanted to know, for example, how many cinemas there were at the centre of Baghdad. I named some. Child's play, for me, of course. My Iraqi origins were soon confirmed. I had to give up, however, on the idea of reaching Sweden. The German police had taken my fingerprints and explained that these would now be forwarded to all other countries that offered asylum. I could no longer apply for asylum anywhere else. Only in Germany. Any attempt to leave would be a criminal offence. So I've been stuck here since.

If it were only things like this, and that were all, life would be bearable, really. But worse was to follow. Many here were simply afraid of me. Yes, afraid! Even though I haven't beaten up anyone nor joined al-Qaeda nor even the CIA. It all began on 11 September 2001. From that day, Arabs in Europe lost their smile. The media spoke of nothing but 'the Evil from Arabia'. At that tense time, I flew from Munich to Berlin for a few days. An old lady next to me, a Bavarian—no prizes for guessing with that accent!—smiled at me.

'Indian?'

'No,' I replied with a smile, 'Iraqi.'

The smile on her lips froze, turned into a grimace distorted by fear and she quickly averted her eyes. For the rest of the flight, she sat glued—pale and silent—to her seat. You'd have thought she'd seen the Devil! One more word from me and she'd have had a heart attack!

THINKING BACK TO THE NAMES I WAS CALLED, in the East or in the West, I realize that they've always had something to do with India. India—where I've never been, a country I don't know at all. The Arabs called me the 'Iraqi Indian', the Europeans simply 'Indian'. I can live, of course, with being a gypsy, an Iraqi, an Indian, an extraterrestrial, even—why not? What I can't live with is that I don't know who I really am. I know only that I was 'burnt and salted by many suns of the earth', as my Bavarian lover, Sara, always says. And I believe her.

I've realized, meanwhile, that there may be a concrete link between me and India, after all—my grandmother. That has a historical background. When the British came to Iraq at the beginning of the twentieth century, they were then also the occupying force in India. Accordingly, they brought a lot of Indian soldiers with them, who set up camp in the south of our country amid the vast palm forests. Who knows, perhaps my grandmother—originally from the south—met an Indian soldier in the forest once. And I am perhaps the product of the union of two British colonies.

TWO

Writing and Losing

THERE WERE NO WRITERS IN MY FAMILY. You couldn't find a decent book, even—apart from the Koran and the government's annual report. Despite which, at some point, I stumbled upon a room full of books—my brother-in-law Sadiq's library. I was very young when he came to ask for the hand of my sister Karima. He married my sister and I married his books. Sadiq lectured on literature at the University of Baghdad; he was a literary critic and mad about books. The first book I read outside of my texts for school was the one he'd recommended and loaned to me. A translation from Russian—*Selected Poems* by Rasul Gamzatov. Once I'd read it, the bird immediately got hold of me, the books bird. I read as if possessed. Poetry, mainly. And then, one day, I thought of writing my own poems. I dedicated the first to my neighbour, Fatima. I was mad about her. She had no idea. She was very pretty and could have had any number of men. She paid no attention to me. And so my first poem was called 'Sighing'. That's how I began writing. At that time, I was composing poems by the dozen. Later, I began reading and writing stories. Poetry, though, touched me more deeply. Back then, I felt it was the 'lung of life that allows me to inhale and exhale'.

Since then, I've been writing almost daily. I've become a writing machine. For a long time, though, I never thought about *why* I write. Writing was connected to my inner life—it was constantly compelling me to write. Three phases were to emerge, of which I wasn't at all conscious. To begin with, I simply wrote, thinking that by writing I could capture my feelings in words. Writing was a kind of lightning conductor that would protect me from psychological defeats. If a stroke of fate struck, I *wrote* and, in doing so, felt such relief you'd have thought the lightning flashing through my soul now streaked across the paper. Then, I thought I could change the world by writing. Just like a revolutionary but with a pencil instead of a weapon. I believed that for a really long time. Finally, I became persuaded that I could even improve myself by writing.

When I write, I see everything as if for the first time, I try to empathize, to understand anew. I am both the student and the teacher. I teach myself and learn from myself. One day I came up with the mad idea of writing my story. I locked myself in my room, blocked out the external world and plunged deep within to bring, each time, another concealed part of myself to the surface. I discovered myself and the world anew and committed this insight to paper. Is what I write real life? I can't say.

Despite writing like a maniac from such an early age, I didn't for a long time actually put down that story of mine, with its countless people, towns, wars, uprisings, dead people, women and disasters. It wasn't because I preferred poetry to prose. No. Prose, too, I write with a passion. The reason was—my terrible memory.

I can quickly forget many things. An ability I consider a blessing. It is thanks to this that I'm still around. I can't imagine what it would be like if I had total recall. I think I'd have ended my life long ago. Fortunately, then, I have a memory full of holes. The most terrible events fall out of it and never return. I have another ability, another blessing—if something terrible does manage to stick to the edge of my memory, I can embellish it completely and utterly. And, in next to no time, the dirt dissolves and only beautiful—or *beautified*—images remain.

But the price I pay for this blessing is very high. If I want to write about real events, I have difficulty not only in depicting towns or people's appearances. My stories also lack what make stories stories—time, place and action. For it's not just names and people's appearances I forget. In my memory, different points in time get mixed up until, in the end, I can only roughly guess at which year it was. Unity of action and its chronology cease to exist too. Sometimes only disorderly, vague scraps of narrative are all that remain of true stories.

And that's still not all. My notes—meant, actually, to *underpin* my memories—represent a *danger*. I've been afraid to confide important things to my diaries since I became aware of the danger of losing them. I wrote—and write—in them only rarely, which is why I call them my 'monthlies'. An entry once a month. Twice, at most. Not because I didn't feel like writing. But because it wasn't easy to write a new entry.

In Baghdad, where I was born and grew up, I had to hide everything. During Saddam's rule, a single word was enough to cost you your life. That's why I used symbols to write down all kinds of things. I made up my own alphabet with Roman and Arabic letters, patterns and numbers that no one but I could decode.

Later, during my escape through the Arab countries, I used the same technique to survive the police checks, when they searched everything—literally, everything. For those emergencies I'd modified my alphabet by adding colloquialisms from southern Iraq. That way, I could note the names of presidents, their atrocities, their slaughters—unknown acts of resistance, too—without anyone even beginning to suspect anything.

Nowadays, though, the problem is that I can barely decipher that alphabet. Even though it's my invention. The keys to the symbols have fallen through the holes in my memory and so the doors to my notes from those days remain permanently locked. To make matters worse, quite a few pages—through the years and in the course of my escape—have also become illegible, for I always write in pencil, even now.

I can suppress any *thought* of lost writings but my diaries *exist* and they keep reminding me of the loss that can be measured exactly by counting the many pages full of my hieroglyphics.

I've suffered another loss. My writings, I think sometimes, are like gypsy tribes and always disappear into some hole or other. One afternoon I came home to find the worst fate imaginable awaiting me—my father had become a Saddamist. The news made the tears pour from Heaven. Our family home wasn't far from the bus stop. The part of town I was born and grew up in—Madinat al-Thawra, the town of the revolution—was calm. Only the patter of rain. Strange weather passed over the district. The square opposite our house—littered with empty oil and tomato-purée tins, broken schnapps bottles, punctured car tyres and twisted bicycle wheels, and where a donkey lived—filled more and more with water. A small lake had formed outside our house and into it flowed streams from our neighbours' yards. As if by magic, shit, rubbish, rotten food was being pushed up from the seepage pit and pooling—stinking like hell—in front of all our homes. My mother usually greeted me with a tasty meal when I got home. This time, though, it was my manuscripts and books that greeted me, drowning in the dirty water outside the house. Like fallen soldiers, they looking up at me in terror. I was hysterical, as any Iraqi is when panic and disbelief blend.

I went in. 'That was Father,' my sister said.

My relationship with my father was never the same. We grew to hate each other. Were like two strangers. Since that day—I have to admit—I was very hard-hearted about him. The sight of him made me sick. But I'd often felt like that, lately, when I looked at myself or many of my fellow humans. We've all mutated into creatures of the imagination. How else can you explain a state declaring as criminal any act of reading and writing outside the schools and universities? Which is why my father thought it best to destroy my books and my writings. Fortunately, I'd hidden all the banned books beneath the pigeon cages on the roof. So my father ended up destroying only the permitted books he'd found in my room. How was he supposed to know the difference anyway? Illiterate, he was unable to write even his name.

Adding fuel to my father's fears, the Iraqi secret service turned up at our house one day. And put me in prison for eighteen months and four days. Because, at some time, and at some place, with friends who worked for banned political parties, I'd spoken ill of the president and helped distribute flyers. In jail, there was neither pen nor paper. The guards considered such things dangerous. A pen could be used as a dagger, after all. Or to write subversive information.

And so, like all prisoners, I wrote on the walls. Our pens were little stones. I wrote a lot. If the walls had fit, I wouldn't have hesitated to pocket them!

Writing on the prison walls involved a certain danger, though—the guards were constantly checking for banned slogans. The Central Prison, where I was, was full of members of Islamic parties who used the walls just as diligently—to write down holy verses from the Koran. And who'd have dared to erase even a single line of that to write something else? He'd have been labelled an infidel faster than he could blink.

The day came, finally, when I got to write on clean white paper. From one day to the next I'd fallen ill. Due to the damp in the jail, many prisoners suffered from skin diseases. I got a completely new one that made my skin look burnt. Fearing it might be contagious, the officers in the prison had me transferred to al-Rashid military hospital in Baghdad. There, in the ward for prisoners, I was able to persuade the warden to get me a pen and paper. I stayed in hospital for a whole week and wrote non-stop. Wrote, without thinking. The best stuff I've ever written, perhaps. When life confronts you with grief and great confusion, you always write something special.

'You're going back to the Central Prison today,' the prison guard said to me a week later.

'Can I take these pages with me?'

'No!'

'Please! I beg you! You look like someone from southern Iraq. My father's from the south too. Please help me—please!'

'Okay, but don't tell anyone.'

'I won't! Promise!'

He took all my clothes, my underwear too, carefully undid some hems and, then, incredibly skilfully, hid my pages in them. Not even the Devil could have guessed that something was hidden in my clothes.

When I was finally released, I couldn't believe at first that I was free again. There'd been a government amnesty for all political prisoners. I returned home in the same clothes the secret service had taken me away in. Incredible! I was getting to see my family again and they, me. I was overjoyed. And confused. I had difficulty grasping reality. Everything seemed like a dream. My mother gave me a clean set of clothes. Only days later did I ask her, 'Where are my things?'

'What things?'

'The ones I had on when I came home.'

'Oh—they were full of lice and stank like hell. I burnt them.'

I WAS STILL IN BAGHDAD when the next loss hit me. My time in jail was behind me, true, but deep within my soul the memory of it burnt brightly. Life outside the prison walls wasn't very different from inside. I felt that there was no longer a life for me. I imagined that everyone was against me, was spying on me, wanted to be rid of me at the earliest opportunity. I could hardly sleep at night. I crouched until dawn on the roof of our house, watching the street like a hawk, convinced that the police would come for me again. And if, by chance, I was able to sleep, I'd wake up in the middle of the night, bathed in sweat. 'Don't hit me. I didn't do anything! Please—leave me alone! I'm innocent!'

My family feared I was going mad. I was haunted almost daily by this nightmare and desperately wanted it to stop. One night, I locked myself in my room, threw the books and notepads from the shelves into a pile and then sat on top of it. Poured petrol, lit a match and let it drop. The fire spread quickly. Everything round me began to slowly become ash and smoke. It was such a wonderful feeling. I was free. Floating away with every charred scrap, every plume of smoke. Suddenly, there was a crash. My brother'd kicked in the door. Then dragged me away from the fire. The next day I got hold of a map of the world and decided to escape. To another country. Far away.

And I succeeded. I spent a few years in various Arab countries in Asia and Africa until the day finally arrived when I could head for Europe. It was then that the greatest loss hit me. At the Turkey–Greece border. Near Edirne, on the Turkish side. I was travelling with about thirty refugees—Kurds, Turkmens, Persians, Afghans, Arabs, Africans, Pakistanis and a Kurdish people-smuggler. We stopped for a short break on a hill. Suddenly—out of nowhere—the border police were upon us. We ran as fast as we could. In all directions. I was running so frantically that I dropped my rucksack and it rolled down the slope. A policeman, who really could run, arrested me. Nodding at the valley, I tried to tell him that my rucksack was down there. It seemed to interest him very little. He dangled a weapon before me. And then began to beat me. When I came to, I was in a Turkish jail—again—and without my rucksack. It had a few tins of food, the little money I owned and a notepad in which, for three years, I'd been recording all my ideas—three years of poetry between Asia and Africa. What a loss! I think, sometimes, that everything I write now is nothing but what I'd written back then. As if I am rewriting everything I've lost.

My escape came to an end in Germany. Since then, I've been living in Munich mainly. Many of my earlier writings reached me by post—things that friends from Asia, Africa and Europe had kept for me. To prevent further losses, I decided to publish as much as I could. Since I've been in Munich, my reading and writing habits have also changed. Often, I sit in a cafe in town to revise my drafts. Everything was going peacefully until, one afternoon, I had the feeling that a loss was springing up on me again. I was sitting, once again, in a cafe in Schwabing and had the manuscript of a book of poems with me. On the bus, on my way home, I leafed through the pages and was happy with the changes I'd made. Then I got off and went home. My flatmate was at the computer. 'How was work, Rasul?'

'Very good!'

I sat on the couch to look at my changes again. I opened my bag to take out my manuscript. Damn! I must have left it on the bus! No! How, after all my tragic losses, could I do something so stupid and ridiculous? How?

'Who're you talking to?'

'Myself!'

'What's wrong?'

'I think I've left my manuscript on the bus!'

'All your corrections gone? I'm sorry!'

'It's not just the corrections. It's the whole manuscript . . . Gone!'

'Hey, man!' he said, with a grin. 'What century are you in? Why do you think we have these machines?'

'What machines?'

'You've saved everything on the computer here, haven't you? Chill, man!'

'Oh!' I jumped up, mouth and eyes wide open. My friend got up so that I could sit at the computer. I clicked on My Documents, then on 'Rasul Hamid', then on 'Poetry Books' . . . And there it was—'Adams-Station'.

Relieved, I grinned at my friend.

'Thank you, Computer!'

THREE

Priests' Daughters

EVEN IN MY YOUTH, I had a lot of bad habits. But what is 'bad'? What for one person is a bad habit can be for another a perfectly good one. Everyone sees what he wants to or, as it often is, does not want to. So, I have been blessed with many odd habits. I like to smoke—a lot. I drink like a hole in the ground—I prefer beer and vodka. Passionately, and very obviously, I love to stare at women in the streets, especially those with well-rounded arses. I read and write only at night. Like to sleep on sofas or on the floor. Without a thought I'll slap people in the face with the truth (this, understandably, has earned me a lot of enemies).

I don't know how or why I acquired these habits. Not even my most embarrassing but unique one—stealing paper. I don't know any more when I began. It may be a dream that is to blame. A dream that's haunted me since I first was able to think. An ancient temple, a thousand years old, perhaps even before the Common Era, decorated with Babylonian, Old Egyptian and Greek sculptures and paintings. From behind a column, I spy on the priest's daughter and the muses as, with bare bosoms, they pray to the gods at the sacrificial altar. I look at their breasts, round, small and firm. When the prayer ends, they scurry outside without a sound. And a tremor goes through me, and I quiver like a palm leaf in a thunderstorm. I creep to the altar, steal a sheet of the sacred temple paper, sit on the floor in front of the fire and begin to write. I can no longer remember what. But I know that since that day—and that dream—I have wanted to do nothing but write. And ever since, this unspeakable paper-stealing curse has weighed heavily on me.

Perhaps my vice began in Baghdad, with Fatima, our neighbour. She had a round face, long blond hair—like the golden sun—and little apple breasts. She wore bright, colourful clothes, patterned with roses and other flowers. Whenever she went to the roof in the afternoon to hang up the washing, my hungry gaze would follow. I'd wait for her to hang up each item, to raise her arms as she did so, and then stare at her bosom moving up and down like that of the priest's daughter in my dream.

Fatima and her bosom aroused in me the urge to write and drove me to my first paper theft. Because of her, I stole paper from my father. Not that he was a writer! No, he just sold dates at the bazaar. If he bought paper, it was only to wrap his customers' dates in. From the staff at the city administration, who stole old official documents and sold them to traders like my father. I should actually say I stole the paper from my mother—for, in truth, it was her job to sell the dates. All my father did was procure the goods. My mother then sat for hours at the bazaar with the funny name—Souk al-Aora, or the

One-Eyed Bazaar—only a few metres away from where we lived. She worked all day, came home exhausted. Her clothes sticky and dirty. Whereas my father hung around the bazaar cafe all day long in his nice, clean clothes and then came home in the evening only to take the day's earnings from my mother. And because he was the man, the shop was *Hamid's*—and not *Selwa's*.

So I'd steal paper from the shop as soon as that trembling hit me. Which was any time I spotted Fatima on the roof. Throughout this time, I wrote the first lines of my life on the blank side of stolen state supplies.

Fatima, however, knew none of this and remained completely unattainable. I felt exactly as the venerable Rilke: 'I want a blonde girl, with whom to play. Wild games.' Poetry without a patina. Oh, how I'd have liked to play wild games with her but I hadn't the slightest hope. In Baghdad, especially in our part of town, al-Thawra, where most of the people were from southern Iraq, everyone was brown- or black-haired. So a blonde was a queen, a one-eyed woman in the kingdom of the blind. At sixteen, Fatima married a thirty-year-old businessman with a stomach that matched his bank balance.

After Fatima, my life was like a desert. Nothing seemed to happen. In Baghdad, in the 'ordinary'—or, to be precise, poor people's—part of town, where the houses stand very close and traditional ways and customs are very much alive, it isn't easy to arrange to meet a girl. You can't just go for a walk with a woman. For that, you have to visit certain places in the town centre, and that only works with women who are public officials or students. They can, at least in part, move freely. With young women who are neither studying nor working in some form or other, it is completely impossible. They have to stay at home. And in al-Thawra, that sort of girl is as common as bread in a bakery. And that's why a unique form of language developed between adolescent boys and girls—the wink-of-the-eye and nod-of-the-head language.

It works like this. The boy goes out for a walk. The girl sits outside her front door or stands at the window. The boy looks at the girl. If she returns his look, gently and somewhat embarrassed, often also smiling imperceptibly, the boy winks at her. This means 'I like you.' If the girl is still smiling, the boy knows it has worked. He walks on, relaxed, along other streets, before returning to the girl. If she's still there, he turns his face to the right or the left. This means, 'Follow me!' Now, one of three things can happen. Either she follows him until they've left the neighbourhood and can speak to each other and agree, if possible, to meet for longer. Or she throws a piece of paper at him on which she's noted the time and place of a possible rendezvous. Or she nods at her bosom. This means, 'Come closer!' If so, the boy goes for another stroll so that no one can see what he's planning. When he then goes past the girl for the third time, he keeps his ears pricked for she's about to whisper the time and place of their rendezvous.

This third happened to me one summer afternoon

with a girl whose name I never learnt. She had wonderful black eyes and gorgeous, big breasts. She lived in another part of town, about thirty minutes' walk from ours. She whispered to me, 'Tonight, at midnight, on the roof.' I spent that whole afternoon and evening nervous and excited and waiting for my writing urge to kick in. I even sneaked out to the bazaar for a few sheets of paper from the shop. That night, I walked round her neighbourhood, strolling past her house every half hour or so, looking up at the roof. I couldn't wait for her to appear up there and nod to me. Shortly after midnight, she finally turned up and signalled at me to climb up and join her. The house was only a few metres high and had enough windows to make the climb easier. It took me a while, though, for I had to keep making sure that no one spotted me.

Finally, standing on the railing, I spotted her—smiling—next to a pigeon cage. She had an incredibly attractive dress on. Or was it a nightdress?—she was half naked. The wall round the roof was about six feet high. When I jumped off, there was a loud thump. And almost immediately, from below, an angry voice screeched, 'What's that? Who's there?' Suddenly, the girl began to run in circles like a madwoman, and shout, 'Help! Help! A thief! He's stealing the pigeons!' Completely thunderstruck, I stared at her, unsure of what to do. 'Run, stupid!' she hissed at me finally, 'Get out of here!'

In one leap I landed onto the neighbour's roof which was a little lower. And from there down to the street. And then, swift as an arrow, off towards my part of town.

Behind me, I could hear furious voices. I glanced back once and saw a crowd of men and boys running after me. Some even waving knives and sticks. I galloped through the streets like a horse gone wild but couldn't shake off the mob. Only once I'd reached my neighbourhood did I dare turn round again. Nothing! Thank God! Sweaty and exhausted, I made my way home. Never again did I return to that district.

Despite that adventure, new attractions sprang up to tempt me and to make me surrender to my mad urge to write. The women in the streets grew more and more seductive with each passing day and my temple dream refused to go away. I continued to steal paper from the shop and to write, until the day came when I had to leave behind the women of Baghdad, Baghdad itself and the date paper.

I REACHED AMMAN. Not as a holidaymaker but as a refugee. It was a difficult place for a refugee but one always finds a way. Amman was a small town though its gentle hills and mountains made it seem bigger. You were always going uphill or downhill. Going up, you felt that someone was clinging to your arse and pulling it back, so you had to stick your neck out. Going downhill, though, you felt the complete opposite; as if, with all their might, someone was pushing your arse forward. In this uphill-downhill town, I finally succeeded in finding a job. In a cosmetics factory, a little outside town. Removing the wet soap curds from the machines, laying them out in the sun to dry, then gathering them up and taking them back to the machines.

The factory was co-owned by a few businessmen. British, they were. One of Iraqi descent. It was also full of beautiful women. The most beautiful of all, Suad, had a breathtaking arse and an almost divine bosom. She worked at one of the machines to which I took the dry curds. My very first day at work, and the urge to write came upon me again, especially when I watched Suad secretly undo the top button of her blouse and then strut up and down before the manager, showing off her cleavage. At such moments, I felt as if I'd returned to a distant past, to the temple, to the priest's daughter, to her bosom. The same tremor, the same quiver, all over my body. The desire to write grew boundless but had not the tiniest bit of paper. On a table I noticed a small parcel—falafel wrapped in paper. It belonged to Suad. On the spur of the moment I took the paper. It was my favourite writing paper in Amman.

I was soon good friends with Suad. She told me she also wanted to write but just for herself. She was from Palestine but had Jordanian citizenship. Her family had to leave Palestine in the forties when Israel began to exist on the map. Suad's father fought for some banned Palestinian organization that wanted to free Palestine from the Israelis. One day, he was found dead in the street, along with his eldest son. Suad had just turned two. His mysterious death remained unexplained. Suad didn't like talking about it though she told me once that the Jordanian government was responsible. 'This government is a disgrace!' Immediately after her exams, poor Suad had to begin working at the soap factory. To keep herself and her mother afloat. Of her dream of becoming a lawyer, she simply said, 'I'll have to forget about that!'

It soon became clear to me that I'd fallen in love with Suad and her fate. A close friendship grew between us. We began going out, mostly to the cinema, and spent a lot of time together. We even wrote poems to each other. I never showed Suad my most important poems from that period, though, for they'd been inspired by her body. And they'd been written in the grip of that indescribable tremor and quiver. I didn't say a word about that either, of course. I simply rejoiced at every day that let me see her sad black eyes.

You can imagine how much paper I used up. I wasn't in a position to buy it, of course. My salary was just about enough to live on—where was I to find the money for paper? I got it from the bins or from the many falafel or kebab stands. Once, I even pinched a whole pile from a snack bar when the waiter stepped into the kitchen.

I wrote for more than seven months, almost daily. It's not as if that in any way means everything was okay. I could no longer remain in Jordan. True, I did have a six-month residence permit but—like all Iraqis who came to Jordan in the nineties—I didn't have a work permit. I had to hide whenever the factory was inspected. Jump over the factory wall and run—as far as possible, as quickly as possible. After your first six months in Jordan, you have to pay the government a dollar per day or be deported to Iraq. But who can afford that?

I'd passed the six-month mark long since. Suad was very sad when I left Jordan but I was sadder still. How I would have liked to tell her I loved her but my courage abandoned me. And so, I left Suad in her substitute homeland and set out to find one for myself.

My poems for Suad and her poems for me I left with her, as my farewell gift. But those I'd written secretly, on falafel and kebab paper I took with me, of course. During my six-day trip, by bus and ship from Asia to Africa, I leafed through them again and again and every word reminded me of my beloved Suad. I wrote her a long letter in which I vowed my love for her. I kept it with me for a long time until, one day, like in a romantic film, I put it into a bottle and threw it into the Mediterranean. Did it ever reach its addressee?

I landed in Libya. Or, to be precise, I landed in Benghazi. A small seaside town, it didn't have a lot to offer other than the sea and numerous beaches—in terms of women, I mean, of course. True, there was a nice selection from Asia and Africa, even Europe, especially Romania, but it wasn't easy to speak to them, let alone touch them. I think that if the government had permitted it, the men would have hung signs on their women: 'Haram—Danger! Don't touch!' On Fridays, you felt like you were in the Sahara. Not a woman to be seen in the streets. Wherever you looked, nothing but believers in a hurry, keen not to miss Friday prayer. In the evenings, too, it was as if the women had all been blown away, except a few foreign girls who, almost always, were accompanied by a man. As usual, there were also a few whores, foreigners mostly, especially from Morocco.

In Benghazi, my hobby of 'looking at women' developed into a science, the theory at its root being what I called 'the analysis of female arses'. With Hasan, a fellow countryman, I hung around Tibisti, the beach in the centre of town, to view the women out for an afternoon walk. In next to no time we'd identified the crucial differences between the different types of arses and arrived at the conclusion that a particular arse could easily be attributed to a particular nationality. Big, curvy arses were Libyan or Egyptian. This, in my opinion, was because of the large amount of noodles and beans traditionally eaten in those countries. Small, firm asses, on the other hand, were Tunisian and Moroccan. Because, as Hasan supposed, those women moved about a lot and had to work as hard as men. Small, broad and slightly flabby asses—on very thin legs, often—were Sudanese or Somali. Perhaps because of starvation, and the merciless sun. Those on firm, fleshy legs were Mauritanian because . . . Well, why do you think? Our theory was hardly likely to play a significant role in the wider field of international science. But Hasan and I had great fun with it. And that was all that mattered.

As if that weren't enough, I finally had a bit of luck with work—and not just with my depleted escape fund.

Right away, in the first few months, I found a position as an Arabic teacher in a primary school. I was kept busy all day every day until a priest's daughter suddenly stood before me in the form of Jasmin, the new English teacher, who instantly caused my now-almost-abnormal compulsion to write to flare up again. This time it was paper carefully removed from the centre of the students' exercise books when they handed them in to be corrected. From each, I took exactly one sheet.

After one particular dream, I desperately needed paper. The dream had made me tremble really fiercely. There it was again—the temple, and round me the priest's daughter and my muses, Fatima, Suad and Jasmin, who, item by item, were removing their clothes and sliding them gently across the ground for me to write on. That night, I crept into my colleague's room—a maths teacher—and pinched paper from his notebook.

Jasmin was from a very traditional family. She was already twenty-four and her mother was horrified that she wasn't married yet. It wasn't long before I heard that a teacher was asking for her hand. I was relieved to have a bit more distance between us. It wasn't that I didn't like Jasmin. On the contrary, I liked her a lot. I was living, though, in constant fear of someone discovering what we were up to. For we were meeting twice a month at the home of her married sister; she was aiding and abetting us by making her home available to us. There, we did all kinds of things to each other. I even wrote a poem on her body once, with lipstick. Unlike with Suad, I let Jasmin read almost all my poems, including those I'd written about her body on the very paper I'd removed from books at school.

In the end, she went to her husband a virgin. As the customs of this country demand. 'A woman must enter marriage as a virgin.' That had been clear to me from the very beginning and I had to take bloody good care that she remain one. It had also been clear to me from the very beginning that our relationship didn't have a future. Jasmin's family would never have agreed to their daughter going to a foreigner, an Iraqi no less, with nothing to his name but a few poems. Several times already, I'd heard of accidents involving foreigners in relationships with the locals. I still remember how the teachers at school once sat together, discussing such a case. A neighbouring school had been witness to a tragic accident a few months before. A music teacher, a Moroccan called Malik, had been murdered. The culprit was never found, no doubt because the police never looked for him. The head teacher said he'd seen the dead man with his own eyes, lying on the ground outside the main door of the school, covered in blood. With a bullet in his head. Shortly before that, another rumour had gone round—Malik had slept with Leila, the chemistry teacher. Soon after the tragic incident, Leila had married someone important. A member of the president's personal army.

So far, so good. Jasmin got married too. My urge to steal paper faded and my contract at the school drew to an end. I had to look for another job. And so, I set out for another town.

TRIPOLI WAS BIG. Very big. In the beginning, I often got lost in the old parts of town, the bazaars and pedestrian zones. The atmosphere wasn't bad, though. You could move about freely, even talk to the women. What's more, the streets were full of foreign women. Any number of whores in the hotels, clubs and other city-centre locations. Usually foreigners, like the underlings of the local pimps.

It took me a while to find work in this big city. First, at a pizza place, then at a beach cafe where I could also sleep at night. From morning till evening, I had to serve the customers with tea or juices and run one film after another on the video recorder. The cafe closed in the evening but a few men would still be sitting, waiting for me to pop in a porno. That was my job, and the men were dealers, junkies, thieves, fences, gays, foreigners and men who had nothing to do all day but watch films at the cafe. Indian films by day. Porn by night.

Things weren't going especially well for me at the time. I desperately wanted a new job but it wasn't easy. The country was full of foreigners who were ready to do anything and that too for hardly any pay. Then, one day, the cafe owner said I could stay in an apartment in a newly constructed building in the centre of town. I was relieved to not have to spend another night at the cafe. There, I couldn't sleep until very late but I still had to wake up early. And it was never really quiet. Often, I couldn't sleep a wink because of the cries and groans of the gay men, trying—at night and very close by—to satisfy their urges. The poor gays—often, they allowed the worst sort to mount them and were then surprised when the same ones beat them up or did who-knows-what to them. Each morning at eight, I had to open the cafe and help my gay Egyptian colleague Jamal to tend his wounds from the night before. And so the apartment in the newly constructed building was my saviour though it was only a tiny room, lit by only a bulb in the ceiling. In it lived four other foreign workers—one from Chad, one from Tunisia, one from Egypt and one from Syria.

Sadly, I was there for only two days before I had to flee. But not because there was only one toilet for twenty people or because the apartment was crawling with lice. No, no, it was because my Syrian flatmate had fucked up. The very first night we'd all been sitting together, he'd boasted, his chest swelling with pride, 'We have a world-class porno here!'

'Oh no—I'm sick of stupid porn flicks!'

'I'm talking of a real one—a *real* porno!'

'What?'

'First, you have to promise you won't breathe a word about this. Not a word outisde these four walls!'

'I promise.'

'Good! Now we just have to wait until midnight!'

At midnight, the Syrian removed a brick from the

wall. 'Let the show begin!'

One after the other, we peeped through the hole in the wall. On the other side were the landlord's daughters in their bedroom. By the time it was my turn, they were lying on the bed, right in front of the hole, and pleasuring each other in the most exhilarating way. The Egyptian explained that they'd removed a brick too and were equally pleasured in sharing with us the mysterious things they got up to at night. Things continued like this for another half hour before one of them got up and put their brick back. My flatmates did the same. Lights out. Show over.

The next day, at work, I could feel the urge to write rising in me again and my heart beginning to beat faster. I sat at a table, grabbed a bunch of receipts from the cafe and began to write, feverishly. That day, I wrote a lot.

In the evening, when I got home, exhausted, an unpleasant surprise awaited me. A crowd of people were standing with the police outside the building. 'Are you the new guy here?' a resident from the first floor asked me softly.

'Yes, what's happened?'

'Piss off quick! They've discovered it!'

'Discovered what?'

'The hole!'

Thereafter I lived as if on a ghost ship. I drifted aimlessly from one job to another, from one town to another, from one country to another, from one escape to another. Women came and went, even writing abandoned me for a long time. It's true that I tried from time to time to commit a few lines to paper but what was missing was the passion. Nor did I feel the urge to steal paper—there was no need for it now. After the peephole incident, my temple dream had suddenly faded away. Only a considerable time later, in Achaea in Greece, did it surface again.

ACHAEA, ABOUT AN HOUR FROM THE TOWN OF PATRAS, was a tiny village. I'd never wanted to go there, nor live and work there. I'd been camping in Patras when I had the thought of going to Achaea. After several failed attempts to reach Italy illegally from Patras, and after spending all my money, I began to look for a job in this part of the world. One day, I heard from a refugee that there were a lot of gypsy traders in Achaea and they were looking for men to help carry their carpets. Without a moment's thought, I headed in their direction.

I lived with six other men in a flat in an old building at the edge of the village. Two rooms. No electricity, no water, no toilet. We fetched water from a next door, we used candles. For our toilet—we went beneath the sky, outside the village. But at least I was earning, and that would keep me going for a while.

My job was to stand in the village square from morning till evening, waiting for someone to ask for a carrier to load his lorry with carpets. I transported carpets produced in a variety of countries: India, Persia,

Arabia—wherever carpets are still produced. I needed neither language skills nor any special training to know what I had to do. And the people explained with whatever gestures it took what I needed to understand.

You couldn't miss the gypsy presence in this village —strings of garlic on the doors and the cautious, if not wary, behaviour round strangers, especially of the gypsy women with their brightly coloured dresses and lots of jewellery. When it came to the women, a stranger could very quickly be in serious trouble. You weren't permitted to speak to them under any circumstances. They liked to go for an afternoon walk along the village streets but always under the beady eyes of the gypsy men. Any approach by a stranger was made utterly impossible. The menacing muscles and big strong hands of their escorts stifled any hint of a wish on my part to approach those pretty women.

I did manage to meet one of them, though. This is how. If there were no carpets that needed to be carried, I carried all kinds of other things. And so, one day, an old lady came up to me and gestured to me to accompany her home. There, a young girl was waiting, wearing a bright house frock. The old lady left me with the girl in the yard and sat down on a chair at the front door. I looked at the girl curiously. She was about twenty, well built and with the kind of flaming beauty you find only in gypsy women. With a few words and many gestures, she tried to explain what I had to do. I was to help her rearrange the furniture in the bedroom—the bed was to go in the corner, the wardrobe beside the window . . . But I could hardly concentrate on the job. With every move, I could peep into her coffee-coloured cleavage. Spotting my nervousness, she began to play a dangerous game—she raised her house frock and tied it round her hips in such a way that I could see more than half of her muscled legs. The colour of chocolate, they were. A wild, highly erotic vision. We worked very slowly and without a word. Sometimes, we touched when we both reached for the same piece of furniture. Each time it happened I felt my heart beat faster, a mad horse galloping away. The job could have been done in fifteen minutes. But we took almost an hour. The old lady noticed. She said something to the girl and then the girl began to work faster. The old lady turned round her chair so that she could watch us. Which is why my job, sadly, was soon done.

This girl whose name I didn't know let loose a hurricane in me. I began to tremble. My vice returned in full force. I noticed how it drew me to a carpet shop. At the entrance was a gigantic container and, beside it, a heap of yellow and white paper that had been used to wrap carpets. I grabbed some quickly, as much as I could, and ran.

I ended up with what you could call 'writing diarrhoea'. That night, the dream attacked me again. I wrote as if possessed, and every time I saw a gypsy woman—*any* gypsy woman—my whole body shook like a bee sucking nectar. I stole paper from almost every carpet shop but didn't see the girl again. Whenever I passed the house I saw the old lady on her chair—but the girl . . . ?

I rode the writing dragon for about a week, a very exciting and successful week, given the long bout of writing constipation that preceded it. I wrote a number of poems and I wrote them for all gypsy women. The fiery girl, though—whom I labelled, in my passion, 'a gypsy priest's daughter'—had almost an entire collection dedicated to her.

As suddenly as it had arrived, the trembling stopped. No earthquake, no dream, no paper raids. The gypsy muse eluded me too, as a butterfly would the winter frost. I decided to remain in Achaea no longer. I'd saved enough to keep me going for a little while. And so I returned to Patras, from where my journey would continue.

I REACHED GERMANY. In Passau—a small town on the border between Germany and Austria, at the foot of the Bavarian Forest mountains, where the Danube becomes two rivers richer—the dream caught up with me.

I discovered many things there, including a totally new ideal of female beauty. Until then, I'd only known what I called 'the cow beauty'. As you can perhaps guess, the 'cow beauty' looks like a well-fed, well-nourished and happy dairy cow living a tranquil life on some grassy meadow. She is as strong and fleshy as the Greek goddess Aphrodite, her role model. To this category belong Arabian, Turkish and Greek women as well as many others of Mediterranean origin. The new ideal I got to know in Passau was 'the goat beauty'. Such a woman seems emaciated—even famished—to me. As good as no stomach; thin, strung-out legs; firm, little breasts; and a tiny, barely visible arse. Much like a goat back home. This I understood to be the Western ideal of a desirable woman—flaunted, as it was, in every magazine, on every TV channel and on every billboard.

Passau seemed to me a wonderful town with its three rivers, its old town, its narrow streets and—despite their goat-like arses—its beautiful women. I lived in an asylum seekers' home, not far from the town centre, in a room I shared with three other men. Once a week, I received a food parcel from the state. Funny-smelling sausage, colourful hard-boiled eggs, bread and juices. Sometimes, there were also fish fingers but they didn't have much to do with fish. I also received sixty marks a month as pocket money from the state or, to be precise, the Foreigners' Registration Office. From the very first moment, I hated that place. The strangest people worked there, bespectacled 'Darwin-type' creatures. They didn't like me, I didn't like them. Enemies from the outset. Why? I don't know. But I do know that they always demanded I obey them. But I didn't want to. 'Off you go!' a female staff member snapped at me once, 'I don't have any time for you right now!'

'Don't speak to me like that!' I shouted back. 'I don't work for your mother.'

'How dare you!' she screeched. 'You won't be getting

any money from us this month.'

The sixty marks kept me in cigarettes for a week, just about. And I wasn't permitted to work. So I couldn't earn my keep, however much I might have liked to.

The worst thing was that, in this town, my temple dream resurfaced. The very first day, that strange trembling came over me again and I felt the urge to write. The streets of this town were full of priest's daughters and muses, some of whom would stretch out half naked on the riverbanks, in the sun, or dance, light-footed, across the squares. Not short of reasons for my pathological paper raids, I descended, greedily on every waste-paper container I could find, be it in a residential complex or in the municipal recycling depot. The people in this town, like many others in the country, have (as I was later to discover) a variety of bins at their disposal—one for glass, one for plastic, one for residual waste and so on. You'd almost think it was a well-stocked supermarket, not a waste-disposal site.

These paper raids increased when I met Olga. She was twenty-five, a Russian of German descent. During the Third Reich, her Jewish grandparents had fled to Russia and died there. Olga later decided to return to Germany, as a former Russian and, now, a German Jewess. I met her in a cafe in Passau. She appealed to me though she was, if anything, a 'goat beauty'. The heart ignores beauty ideals and other such conceits. We liked each other right away but, sadly, everything was against us. She was from a Jewish family and I from a Muslim one. To top it all, she was still married to a Russian. An alcoholic. He sometimes hit her so much that I had to deal with her bruises. Nonetheless, she didn't want to leave him. For their child's sake. She often said, quietly and sadly, 'If the Russians ever find out I'm with you, you're dead.' This period was so full of paper raids and poems that I've lost all measure of where, when and how many I wrote.

I was glad to get a residence permit in the end. To be officially entitled to political asylum. And so I decided to take my leave of Passau, Olga and the town's half-naked women. I left alone. Saying goodbye to Olga was hard for me. Though, again, it was entirely clear to me that the relationship was in no way possible.

Today I live in Munich, far from my previous towns. This city is so unique that I can hardly bear it sometimes. As beautiful as a rose, as a plastic rose. Like a private hospital—totally fucking clean and expensive. I hate the winter here, when the residents' faces make you think they've all just failed an exam. In summer, however, I never want to be away for very long. Suddenly, the town dresses differently. Or, rather, undresses. Like the women along the Isar. And it flirts with you. Like the women with their miniskirts and tender flesh, the colour of milk. And though the Foreigners' Registration Office and the police in this town have, honestly, never allowed me to lead a calm life—the police used to harass me the minute they'd spot my black hair and brown face out and about in the street—I've experienced my temple dream here again, in all its intensity. Because this town is so full of shapely Bavarian ladies with incredibly round breasts and curvy arses—and this, in the land of the 'goat beauties'. And so my paper raids continue here too.

I'd noticed right away the unusual newspaper boxes—on legs—located on many a street corner. You can take a paper and simply put the required amount of money in the slot. If I'd had the money, I could just as well have bought a proper notebook. Given, however, that my financial means were, as ever, more than just 'limited', I had no choice but to succumb to my urge and *steal* the newspapers and use the narrow margins to write on. I even dipped into the briefcase of my new Bavarian girlfriend. But barely had I opened it when . . .

God, how embarrassing! I'd been caught red-handed for the first time. Sara demanded an explanation. From the beginning. Starting with the temple and leading to her briefcase. From then on, she—silently—supported my habit. In her own way, naturally. By leaving her briefcase out on the table and strutting off to the bedroom. Like some priest's daughter.

FOUR

Talking Walls

I FREQUENTLY WONDER about the fate of languages, given that they entered the world as a curse. God's curse, when He was angry with humanity for trying to reach Him through the Tower of Babel. Babel isn't far from my home town Baghdad, just a hundred and twenty kilometres away. My mother was born there. From that point of view, I suppose you can say that I have Babylonian blood in my veins. Shortly after I heard the story of the tower for the first time, my family paid a visit to my grandparents in Babel. I, of course, was dying to see the tower. My grandfather said, 'The Tower of Babel hasn't existed for a long time. But if you look very closely, you can still see it.' It was a long time before I undesrtood what he meant by 'look very closely'.

A good friend of mine, a student of English philology in Baghdad, wished to continue his studies in Australia. He told me that he thought the tower was no more than a symbol for the various languages. In a letter to me, he asserted that the tower had never really existed and cited several pieces of evidence to support this view. But the curse of the tower was to dog him. As far as Australia, almost, where he hoped to land, illegally. He was swallowed up by the sea. To me, it doesn't matter whether the tower existed. Whether humanity had indeed brought God to the point where He finally shifted His arse and used His power against them. The one important thing was that the tower was the reason for human beings to want to be able to record and write things as well as to speak languages. Why? Quite simple: if people have many languages, they write in order to protect their own as well as to communicate with others. I can easily imagine that—as is written in the Bible—in the beginning was the word; the word scrawled on a stone in the tower by a madman following the curse: 'I am the forefather of all authors to come.'

Perhaps as a result of my Babylonian blood, I began to scribble on walls from an early age. Not to protect my language, though. But to annoy older people. Back then, I didn't know the lines by Heinrich Heine: 'And it wrote and wrote on the white wall letters of fire; and it wrote and disappeared.' Nonetheless, I wrote and disappeared. In my intermediate-school years, I adorned the walls with provocative indecencies: 'The head teacher's an arsehole.' 'The literature teacher's fucking the cleaner.' 'The imam is gay.' 'The president is fucking everyone.' And observed with relish how the teachers, the police and the government officials searched the school for suspects. That was my game. I'd played it for a while before it came to a sad end. The government arrested a large group of boys from our district, labelled them 'dangerous', 'suspicious'. The boys never came back. At first, I thought they'd return all right. Then it was rumoured that they'd admitted, under torture, to writing those slogans. Never again did I write another sentence on the wall. Even today, I'm plagued by the thought that I was responsible for those boys leading a life in prison.

Fate had possibly played the same game with me. At the age of nineteen, I was put in prison for a similar reason. Where there was any number of walls to write on. Nothing but walls. A window was an alien concept. As were the sun and women. You could only guess that the sun shone somewhere out there. On the dark side of the Earth, the first line of verse I read was on the wall of my first cell: 'Prison is, for me, an honour; the shackle, an ankle bracelet; and the gallows, the heroes' swing.' Its author must have lost all hope. I grew frightened. Back then, I had no intention of ending up as a hero at the gallows. A year later, I wrote the same line in another cell and thought nothing of it. Simply anything and everything was written on the walls. You could spend a lot of time exploring the worldview of the various prisoners, their ethnic or religious affiliations. 'Workers of the world, unite!'—a communist. 'Free Kurdistan!'—a Kurd. 'May God protect the believers'—some religious person. 'Come, Holy Imam al-Mahdi, and save the earth!'—a Shi'ite. 'I want to go back to my mother.'—someone like me, with no idea why he was there.

Not all holy men were present on these walls, though. Joseph—sent from God—was the wall star of this prison. 'God, free me as you freed Joseph from prison!' This Joseph was everywhere, as if he'd been the only one God ever sent to earth. The Shi'ites have an imam known as al-Kadhim. He was poisoned in prison.

His name could be found everywhere too. You could hardly overlook the fact that the person who'd written al-Kadhim's name had had enough, with life or what was left of it. And so I spent my time analysing the sentences on the walls.

Later, I discovered a new game. I studied the inscriptions to try and find out how long their authors had spent in prison. Many wrote their date of arrival on the wall as soon as they arrived. Very few also had a second date. Of their release, perhaps? In most cases, though, there was only the one. I memorized certain styles of lettering and looked for similar ones in other cells. For, in the course of my time in prison, I went from one cell to another. And so, in time, I discovered that the inscriptions without a second date were generally by the Shi'ites and Kurds. This set loose a boundless fear in me for I, too, was a member of a Shi'ite family. In the end, I had the good fortune to be allowed to see the light of the sun again—after eighteen months and four days.

Since my rebirth I've barely written on the walls. Instead, I read more than ever what others have left behind. I don't know why. After my release, it hardly made sense to besmirch the walls. In my eyes, things had changed. I thought only of fleeing now. And so I battled my way to Jordan. And from the harbour town of al-Aqaba, I made it by sea to Egypt. On the dirty, old ship were hundreds of Egyptian workers, taking home new TVs, video recorders and clothes. A few Iraqis, too, wanting to get as far away as possible from their homeland.

The ship's sides were covered with inscriptions. I spent the hours not looking out to sea but reading all the scrawls. The most beautiful, and the most heartbreaking, was: 'Welcome to Africa. He who enters is lost. He who gets out, reborn.'

The inscriptions were constantly changing. Once, I found my name everywhere. It was in a village on the border between Chad and Libya. The village of the Garar tribe. For a brief while, I found work there. The Muslims from Chad were desperately looking for someone to teach their children the Koran. True, there were a few in the tribe who knew Arabic but the village elders felt that a real Arab would make a better teacher. The village didn't have a school. Only a tent. The children sat on the ground. A board, held up by dowels and stones. A chair for the teacher. That bothered me less, actually. What bothered me more was that, from the very first day, everyone laughed at my name. The children, too, grinned cheekily and followed me with shouts of 'Mister Rasul'. After my first walk through the village, I understood part of the puzzle. My name was everywhere, on every wall—in the valley, on the hill, on every stone. The men with me explained, mysteriously, that the name had been written all over the village for a long time and hadn't anything to do with me. To me, it seemed strange. The head teacher reassured me with a smile, 'The people in this village believe that, some time in the future, a hero will come. He will be called Rasul and he will change the world.'

'Are you serious?'

'It's true. But it has nothing to do with you—the hero is from Chad, not Arabia.'

I didn't believe a word. The inscriptions seemed to point, at least, to a glimmer of hope. Nonetheless, 'Rasul' was to appear more and more on the stones in the valley. I thought nothing of it. Hero, after all, isn't necessarily the worst thing I have been called. When, after three months, I was to return to Tripoli, I took my leave of these people who had been so good to me. The head teacher accompanied me to the car and said, with a smile, 'Now I can tell you why your name is everywhere. It has nothing to do with heroes, nor with you.'

'Then—?'

'Some time ago, we had an Arabic teacher from Libya. His name was Rasul too. The boys in the tribe liked him a lot, spent all their free time with him. When he left, some of them—still longing for him—wrote his name everywhere.'

'Was he that good?'

'Yes . . . and . . . umm . . . he was gay.'

THE INSCRIPTIONS ON THE WALLS were so different in the East and the West that, sometimes, I couldn't work out whether they were meant positively or negatively. My next stop was Turkey. I had to cross the Greek border illegally, on foot. It was my third attempt, already, that ended on the bank of the Ebrus. Many had lost their lives in it—the 'river of doom', the refugees called it—trying to swim across to Greece. I remember a young Persian who was dragged under by a powerful wave. He never came up for air again. The river can rightly be called an 'international watery grave'. Countless people of many countless countries have lost their bodies and souls to it. To them, I dedicated the following inscription on a tree on the Turkish side: 'This is the River Ebrus, an international watery grave and meeting place of many cultures.'

Each time, I sat on its bank and dreamt of reaching the other side. It was really and truly a curse, this border river. Three times, I was arrested by the Turkish police. The third time, I was sitting beside a tree as our people-smuggler fixed his rubber dinghy. Carved into the tree in Arabic was 'Here is where the sun goes down in the east and rises in the west.' I didn't have the time, sadly, to consider what the author meant by that for a loud voice—'*Durmak, polis*!'—Freeze, police!—tore me from my thoughts.

At the fourth attempt, I succeeded in crossing the river of doom. Nonetheless, I had to return to it. On the Greek side of the river, the police surprised our gang of refugees. They took us to a prison in Komotini. In the dirty, old, damp, smelly prison were jailed a vast number of refugees. Someone had written on the wall, in English: 'Welcome to Istanbul.' I asked a Kurd beside me, 'We're in Greece, aren't we?'

'Yes, we are.'

'So what does this mean?'

'Nothing. I think the police wrote it to let us know that we'll all be deported to Turkey. They're making fun of us.'

'Are we really being deported?'

'Yes.'

'Why?'

'Because they send back all those they arrest before they reach Thessaloniki. If you get beyond Thessaloniki, they send you to Athens.'

'Is that the law?'

'It's a fact!'

I SUCCEEDED—after years of trying—in crossing the Mediterranean and reaching Germany. In Germany, the police sent me to Bayreuth. I stayed there for a while in an asylum seekers' home, full of refugees from different countries. The rooms were between twenty and thirty square metres and meant for four to six people. I slept in a room with three men, also from Iraq. The walls were full of inscriptions and paintings. One of my room-mates told me that on a wall in the next room was a poem that sounded incredibly hopeless and cruel. 'Chronicle of Lost Time', it was called. I went over and read it. It ended with these lines:

In the seventh wound
I sit beside the graveyards

and await my coffin
that passers-by will carry.

I couldn't say a word. Went back to my room. I couldn't believe it. The poem was one of mine. What kind of world was this? No matter how hard I thought about it, I could think of no one who could have written it on the wall. It had to be one of the many friends I'd made on one of my many escapes. I often wrote poems and then gave them to friends to keep safe for me. That day, I knew I'd found the title for my first book of poems.

From Germany, I went on my first journey as a tourist. I'd been on the road for four years but as a refugee. My Bavarian girlfriend Sara invited me to travel to Italy with her. We went in her car—and with a tent—to Verona. A beautiful little town, and the home of Juliet, Romeo's beloved. I was delighted to be able to visit that square steeped in history. The entranceway and the walls of the passage were completely covered with the signatures of lovers from all over the world. I remembered the story of the Tower of Babel. And, suddenly, I understood what my grandfather meant when he'd said, 'Look very closely.' The languages of the world had come together—right below Juliet's balcony. Not because of God's anger but because of love. Lovers wrote their messages in every imaginable colour and their scrawls formed a huge fresco on the wall. At that moment, it occurred to me that there could be Arabic legends too. I looked and found the wonderful words '*Habibti*, *Habibi*'—my inamorata, my inamorato. I found another but that made my mouth fall open with horror. I stood there, rigid. As if a snake had bitten me. There it was, in clear handwriting: 'You evil-doers, what a return awaits you, Hell is your shelter and the journey to it is terrible.'

My girlfriend wrote our names on the wall. 'And what have you found?' she asked me. 'What does this Arabic writing mean?'

'What else, but Love!'

FIVE

Save Me from Emptiness

MY GRANDFATHER'S FACE was like the walls of our house, old and weather-beaten. Like a stone on the beach. Like an eternal sailor. He'd lost his sight but was exceptionally big and strong. So strong that not even a mob of fully grown young men could have flattened him. I, at least, was convinced of that. He said that was his nature. 'One of God's whims—or have you an objection to that?' he'd laugh and ask whenever the subject was raised. He died when I was still at intermediate school.

I can remember one day, even now. I was playing football with my brothers in the yard. I shot the ball at the goal but didn't score. It landed within my grandfather's reach. He picked it up with a grin: 'You're not getting it back!'

'Please, Granda, I'm losing as it is.'

'Do you really want it back? Then you'll have to fetch it! Come on, be men! Try, at least!'

Three of us, boys aged between ten and eighteen. But we couldn't wrest back the ball from that blind man of ninety-eight. He grabbed all three of us with his huge strong arms. We couldn't move. Then he broke out into gales of laughter, 'Come closer to your Granda, closer! I want to smell you!' He did that. Sniff at me, I mean. He often said that my smell reminded him of many people he'd encountered in the course of his eventful life. Especially Jabar, his brother and our great-uncle, whom I'd never met. When my family talked about Jabar, Hussein, the strong man, would grow weak. Hardly would they have started talking about Jabar when he would begin to cry. He included him in his prayers, daily. 'Allah, the Almighty, bring Jabar back to us as you once brought Joseph back to his father, David.' But he wouldn't tell us what had happened to Jabar.

My family believed that Jabar had gone to India, or Iran. But why? It was a long time before I heard more of the story. At the beginning of the twentieth century, somewhere in southern Iraq, Jabar fell in love with a black servant. Her name was Nerzes. She'd been exceptionally pretty. Jabar's father, my great-grandfather, was then the head of our tribe and totally against his son marrying a black servant. But Jabar had no intention of bowing to his father's will and decided, without his father's consent, to take Nerzes as his wife. A few days later, very early in the morning, everyone was rudely awakened by the sound of women screaming. Some of them had gone to the well to fetch water and they'd found Nerzes, dead. Someone must have killed her and left her body there. Jabar got on his horse and sped off in the wind, that same day. No one saw him again. Where did he go, and who killed poor Nerzes? No one from our tribe talked about it, never mind trying to bring the murderer to justice. I am quite sure that only one person could have committed this despicable act—my great-grandfather.

The second person to escape from our family was my humble self, even if there wasn't a woman involved.

It began in the eighties, during the Iraq–Iran war. I can clearly remember my sister leaping under the stairs with tears in her eyes when the alarm went off. It was the first time I'd seen so many planes all at once. My mother thought every existing demon, dragon, snake and evil spirit had come to attack us. I thought so too. The planes were flying very low. I could see the face of a pilot through the windscreen. Missiles were being fired into the air. Detonations, rockets, smoke—wherever you looked. From the military base not far from our district, rockets were being fired at the planes. Their ear-splitting noise made the houses tremble. That went on for a few minutes until the siren howled again.

'The attack is over!' my father declared.

My sister Farah's face suddenly turned white. She rolled her eyes. Then fell, unconscious, to the ground. 'Pour some water on her face!' my father commanded. 'Typical woman! No guts!'

'What's going on?' I asked, bewildered.

'What do you think? War!'

'Who with?'

'With your aunt's arse—Iran!'

We turned on the TV. The newly elected president of Iraq appeared on the screen and said in a pathetic voice:

'A curse on our foe! Death and doom to our foe!' After his speech came the first declaration of war. The speaker began with 'May our foes be cursed,' followed by the song 'Curse, curse, curse'. Finally, he announced another war film—*The Curse of War*.

•

THIS IRAQ–IRAN WAR WAS OVER AFTER EIGHT YEARS but not the other wars. The next one arrived. That was in 1991, when thirty-three countries from all round the world gathered in the Arabian Desert to free Kuwait from an Iraqi invasion. Baghdad was like a ghost town during this war. No light. Only the fear of rockets and bombs and other surprises. I remember the first day of the war. The attack began at midnight. I could hear only the screams of my mother and my sisters as huge detonations shook the house. We ran quickly, hid in my parents' bedroom on the first floor. My mother used clothes to stuff the holes in the window. 'If the Americans use chemical weapons, this will stop the gas from getting in!'

The attack lasted half the night. It was over in the morning. Apart from isolated rifle fire, here and there. Many families used the light of day to flee Baghdad. My father felt we should too. That same day we left for Karbala. One of my brothers, Ilyas, worked and lived there with his wife and children. He'd said on the phone that there were no important military facilities in Karbala. When we arrived, the war was, of course, there too but it was not as noticeable as in Baghdad. My brother didn't live in the town centre but outside, in a district called al-Alaskari. It was huge and at the edge of the Karbala desert. There was no electricity, but we could listen to the terrible news on a battery-operated radio. We were relieved to be outside Baghdad.

In the town centre were the mosques of the holy Shi'ite imam al-Hussein and his brother al-Abbas. Countless pigeons lived in their courtyards. They'd even built their nests beneath the golden domes. It gave me all kinds of pleasure to visit the mosques daily and watch the pigeons, though my family thought I'd become religious. At the time, I did indeed go through what you could call a religious phase. On the way to the mosques, I often sat in the inner courtyard, at the grave of al-Hussein, listening to the prayers, especially of the women: 'May God end this war!', 'Save us, O Merciful One!', 'O God, in the name of your holy imam al-Hussein, bring my children safely back from war!' They cried and then grew calm after their prayers, as if their problems had gone away.

A short time later, the war ended. Kuwait liberated, the Iraqi army returned to Iraq. My family, to Baghdad.

The war was followed by the embargo on Iraq by the victorious powers. The Iraqis therefore went hungry. There was a lack of medicine and many other things. The dictatorship got worse. Resistance seemed impossible. I was arrested for political reasons and later released. There was no path left open for me after that. Just a great nothingness—all over the country.

A kind of illness began to take hold of me. I don't know what to call it, exactly. An unknown poet in the Middle Ages wrote: 'I opened my eyes and when I opened them, I saw many people and yet I saw no one.' I fell into this no-one state, plunged into a great emptiness. And I couldn't get out of it. Only two choices lay before me—to fight this emptiness or to put an end to my life. Heaven and earth were bleak, empty. I decided to leave Iraq. I could no longer bear—in the emptiness of my homeland—to watch life in its sad streets.

My last day in Iraq I spent with Abba and Abd, my childhood friends. I told them of my plans to leave Iraq. Abba and Abd took me by the hand and led me to a square called al-Sade, not far from where we lived. Where there was nothing but yellow soil and where the bin lorries of Baghdad used to be emptied. Once we'd arrived at the square, they said, 'God is certainly in Heaven! Now let's dance for Him!' We danced like madmen. I screamed. Afterwards, I felt as free as a pigeon that had just learnt to fly.

Thereafter, I always repeated the prayer I'd once heard an old man say in al-Hussein mosque. It has remained deep in my heart. The old man claimed it came from Ali Ibn al-Hussein. Ali is the fourth great imam of the Shi'ites. After Caliph Yazid murdered his father and his family and friends in 680, in Karbala, he'd spent the rest of his life sitting in a room and doing nothing but pray. He'd also written a book, *al-Sahifa al-Sajjadiyya*—'the pages of the prostrate one'—containing nothing but prayers. That is why they finally called him 'al-Sajjad'—the prostrate one. I have Ali al-Sajjad and his pages to thank for the one prayer I've uttered in my life: 'God, save me from emptiness!'

THE FIRST STOP ON MY LONG JOURNEY was Amman. But heavenly paths weren't to be found there either; only others that I can't describe so easily. Paths of a particular kind. One of them I call 'access to exile'. The first days you spend in exile are very dangerous. You no longer think with your head but with your heart or, to be precise, with your imagination. Your head is forgotten. You often think of your mother's face or those of your brothers and sisters and your friends. They appear all over the place—in a book, at your work, in the sky. You begin to listen to songs from your native land. At home, under no circumstances would you have behaved like this. The songs you would have dismissed as banal. Food, books, clothes and people from your native land suddenly gain in significance. Exile enhances your view of the place you've left behind.

I think my problem was that I hadn't travelled voluntarily. I wasn't a tourist. Only a refugee. A fleeing pigeon that was completely blind. It was able to fly but it didn't know where to go. I was forced to leave my homeland for ever, that much was certain. But I still didn't know what I would do elsewhere! I had to survive and that was all. My 'access to exile' path was a long path through the emptiness that I had to fight all my life. The longing for your homeland grows fainter with time. The more you penetrate the emptiness of exile in your new life, the more the touched-up past fades. Emptiness, though, is the one thing that remains, your constant companion.

'God, save me from emptiness!'

IN AMMAN, in a bid to battle the emptiness, I tried to make contact with members of the Iraqi opposition. A group of Iraqi politicians and writers in exile met in a cafe in Amman every afternoon. When I came to know them better, I couldn't believe it—more than half had been generals, poets and writers who'd supported the Iraqi dictatorship in the eighties. I'd even seen some of them on TV, reading poems or making speeches in praise of the dictator. On one occasion, a poet who saw himself as an important representative of contemporary Iraqi literature, proudly read a poem he'd published for the king of Jordan in a Jordanian newspaper. He'd previously published several volumes of poetry dedicated exclusively to the Iraqi 'leader' and his wars. I immediately recalled the old Arabic poet: 'And yet I saw no one.' These people had sold out, completely. But what were they up to, in exile? A poet called Akram—with sad black eyes and a loud, deep, broken voice—explained: 'Following the war of 1991, Saddam and his government have grown weak. The Iraqi dinar hasn't been worth a damn since the embargo. That's why, suddenly, many high-ranking military men and intellectuals have gone abroad and joined the opposition. The writers now write for other dictators in other Arab countries and earn a lot of money. They also write for Iraqi opposition parties and earn a second lot of money. The generals receive money from the Americans and other countries that have a problem with Saddam—to ensure that they support the countries in question in their own way, especially against their own opposition, and so on and so forth . . .'

'I don't believe that!'

'Just look at Syria. The dictatorship in Damascus is murdering the communists in its own country but is supporting the communists in Iraq. It's all one big game!'

It's easy to understand that, in such circumstances, I felt no great desire to remain with these people, to be part of this big game. Akram said it was best to go away—to where there were no lies.

'Where?'

'No man's land . . .'

'Where's that?'

'Perhaps in the Bermuda Triangle!'

Akram stayed for a while with his high-ranking 'friends', then he fled, not to the Bermuda Triangle, of course, but to Lebanon. A few years later, I heard that he'd killed himself. He probably couldn't free himself from emptiness, nor fight it. And so he chose the oldest and easiest way out.

I quickly forgot those people and tried to find new paths for myself in Amman. But there weren't many. Working, reading and writing managed to soothe my longing and the need to meet other Iraqis died down. Thus, to some extent, I was able to avoid news from Iraq. For the same reason, I called my family just once a month. In the end, it also helped me to wander, alone, out into the Jordanian desert and to scream. Screaming is the best cure for emptiness but, sadly, an all-too-fleeting one. The emptiness on earth and in heaven weighed on you in Jordan too. Staying was not the best option. The next possibility for me was Libya. There you could at least feel free in the desert as it was so big. And so I bought a ticket and set out on my way without thinking about what I'd actually do there.

'God, save me from empt-i-i-i-i-i-i-i-i-i-i-i-ness!'

IN LIBYA, I decided to flee to the West again. Life in the Arabian Desert under another dictatorship—this time, African—was unbearable. I saw and experienced for myself just how terrible things were. The country consisted of a single man, or a single family, who held all the power and determined the fates of its people. It was a land so filled with the sand of brutality that even a camel would lose its bearings. It would take more than the patience of a camel to be able to bear all that. The patience I had, even—though that clearly wasn't enough.

I no longer wished to stay there. Actually, I no longer wished to stay in any place where pictures of some president or other hung in the streets. The countries in which I was to land up in future I'd divided into two groups—where there were posters of their leaders, like in Libya, and where there weren't. That's the kind of place I wanted to go to. I'd always heard about how that kind of thing existed only in the West. So I began the first stage of my long journey to the western hemisphere.

WE WERE THREE MEN who'd met in Benghazi—a Sudanese, a Libyan and an Iraqi. Izhaq, the Sudanese, wanted to get married, start a family and live in peace. Abu-Agela, the Libyan, wanted to know the mountains and snow and 'a blonde wife, a house in the forest and as much money as possible'. I didn't know what I wanted. Nothing more, perhaps, than to overcome my emptiness and to take myself as far away as possible from any danger.

Izhaq was our people-smuggler. He wasn't a proper smuggler, of course, but a French teacher and a fisherman. 'If I'd known my studies would only be worth the piece of paper my result was printed on,' he'd once said, 'I'd have become a fisherman far sooner.' Because in Libya the level of interest in French was extremely low, he'd been working, since his arrival in Benghazi, as a fisherman on the boat of a Libyan businessman. 'I don't want to stay. This place is killing me,' he said every time I met him.

Abu-Agela, who'd fled from his tribe, no longer wanted to be a grain of sand in the Sahara and laughed at by his tribe. One day, he'd gone with the other boys to the holy stone in the desert—where they met once a week at the campfire to sing and dance. 'It's a wonderful stone! It's said that it was the very first stone and fell from the sky with Adam. It is big, white and shines in the night. Just imagine that—a white stone and the black skin of the boys in the yellow desert! And then dancing and shouting round the campfire to the wild beats of the drum beneath the black sky!'

That day, he didn't go to the stone with the others. 'I saw Ouarde. She lived up to her Arabic name—she was a real *flower*. She looked at me as if I were the most handsome boy in the world. I didn't know Ouarde well but I knew she didn't have a good reputation in the tribe. But she was pretty—very pretty. Everyone said she was doing it with the head of the tribe though he had two wives and eleven children. I was only thinking of having fun with her. But she seduced me. I followed her to a valley far from our village. We hid there and it happened. My first time! A month later, the head of the tribe came to me and said that Ouarde was pregnant. Was claiming that I was the father. I didn't know what to say. When a woman speaks such nonsense, there's nothing to say. All the men had rifles in their hands and were talking about honour. But I knew it was a trick and that the head of the tribe himself was behind it. I couldn't possibly be the father. I'm not stupid. How was she supposed to have got pregnant? I'd only fucked her up the arse! But I had to marry her. There was no other option. Marry her or be shot. Two days after the wedding, I ran.'

Abu-Agela and I stood at the Mediterranean every day and he said the same thing every time: 'It's hard as hell to cross this sea.'

'Look—this ship here? Where's it off to? What do you think?'

'Yes, look closely. Where to? Over there's Italy and over there, Malta. And back there, Holland.'

'But the police?'

Abu-Agela knew Izhaq and he joined us. We sat with our maps daily, planning our escape to Italy. The trip was to begin in Izhaq's boat. We went to the harbour in the evening. It was Friday and, on public holidays, the town was like a desert. Hardly anyone in the streets or at the harbour. We got into the boat. From the sea, I looked back at Benghazi. Its lights disappeared slowly. Suddenly, it was no longer there.

The boat was drifting.

Though I was restless I fell asleep. When I woke up, I found Izhaq staring at me. 'Man, you were asleep for six hours!'

Round us, a deathly hush, the only sound that of the waves splashing against our boat. Suddenly, Izhaq hissed, 'There's light over there!'

'An Italian ship?'

'I've no idea. I'm not a clairvoyant!'

'Shit, it's Libyan!' said Izhaq.

We spent a few unbearable days in the Benghazi harbour prison. If it hadn't been for Abu-Agela and his muscular body, who knows what might have happened! A cell reeking of damp and mould, more than twelve people squeezed in together. All with very special crimes to their names—murder, manslaughter, rape . . . One of them, covered in tattoos, tried to hit on me and Izhaq. Abu-Agela flattened him, then planted himself in front of us like a giant. From then on, we were left in peace. They had their fun in the end, though. Found two other guys for their hot group-sex games. The pair seemed perfectly happy, so Abu-Agela held back and let them be.

In the end, the police magistrate believed our claim—that we had just wanted to go on a little boat trip round Benghazi. Nevertheless, we had to sign a bond that we would never hang around near the harbour. Izhaq lost his job. Following our release, he decided to go to South Africa, this time not by sea but on foot, across the desert. Also illegal, of course. Abu-Agela wanted to go to Tunisia and then onwards from there.

On the day of our release, I went to the beach in the evening and looked at the sky, the sea, the ships and the gulls. I closed my eyes and began to scream with all my heart and soul. I spread my arms like a pigeon would its wings and danced on the beach. Like a wave, or a pigeon that has just been killed. Like a raging camel. Whenever things went wrong, I danced and screamed. Though not exactly a good dancer, I danced with a passion. Like I was Zorba the Greek. I danced whenever I felt I had no paths, no dreams, no hope any more. Whenever emptiness engulfed the world round me. Afterwards, I felt free, new-born. Like a gull for which every route is open. Like an eagle floating in the sky. I danced on the beach of Benghazi, screaming. Then set out on my path home. Home? Where was that? A hole under the stairs of a building—ten square metres, maybe. The landlord allowed homeless people like me to live there for not much money. That night I slept well and woke up having decided to go to Tunisia with Abu-Agela.

'God, save me from emptiness! God, save me from emptiness! God, save me from emptiness . . .'

AT THE BORDER between Libya and Tunisia, in Ras Ajdir, you encounter two different centuries simultaneously. On the Libyan side, you look into the eighteenth or nineteenth century; on the Tunisian, the twentieth. During the journey from Tripoli to Ras Ajdir, we looked out at the landscape through the window of our shared taxi—old cars, old houses, sand, the yellow colour of the country, the faces of sad men. Faceless women. Shrouded in garments, like walking mummies. The disorganized world, the government posters, the pictures of the president, the countless policemen and plastic bags, plastic bottles, tin cans, scraps of newspaper lying at the side of the road. Shortly before we reached Ras Ajdir, we noticed a poster that said 'The yellow desert turned green.'

'See anything green here?' whispered Abu-Agela.

'No.'

'That's Libyan logic for you. Lie, lie and lie again so that, in the end, the yellow desert starts looking green.'

The other side of the world, Tunisia, was completely different. The streets, clean. The women, with faces. And really green spots. Only a few pictures of the president, a few posters. 'In Tunisia,' the taxi-driver explained, 'you can do anything you want except politics.'

'What does that mean?' asked Abu-Agela.

'Women, alcohol, whatever. But never criticize the government. You'll get in real trouble if you do!'

'Okay—thanks for the tip!'

In the capital city, we soon established how right the man was. A glance at the newspaper and you saw nothing but how wonderful the government was! A Tunisian in our old dirty one-dollar hotel told us that politicians or intellectuals who spoke out against the government were arrested in no time at all. 'The same shit again!' Abu-Agela groaned, 'Just not in military uniform but in suit and tie.'

Well, the solution of these countries' problems wasn't the point of our trip. We had problems of our own. We were looking for just one way across the sea to Europe. Abu-Agela tried every day to get to the sea and find a people-smuggler. I stayed in town so as not to waste too much money on these trips. I spent my time on Avenue Habib Bourguiba, looking at women and trying to chat them up. Two weeks passed and we still hadn't found a smuggler to take us to Europe. My visa, though, was valid for only two weeks and—as I was Iraqi—couldn't be extended. Abu-Agela, being Libyan, had a permit for three months. Another two weeks and we still didn't have a smuggler. One night, sitting with Abu-Agela in the hotel room, I heard them roaring. The police. The hotel owners must have tipped them off, told them my visa'd expired.

At the station, the police magistrate explained that I had two options—back to Iraq or back to Libya. Plus, a fine for being in Tunisia illegally. In my wallet, however, was only about sixty dollars. They did without the fine but I had to sign a document saying that I would never return to Tunisia. They wanted to send me back to Libya the next day. I spent the night in a small cell that was old and crawling with lice. My two cell-mates were refugees from Nigeria. We couldn't understand a word of each other's languages. They didn't speak English either, only French. I didn't know a word of French. So we were forced to use sign language. Clearly, they'd been in a boat when the police arrested them. They wanted to get to Italy too. That's all I could understand. I slept and thought of my prayer but I had the feeling, somehow, that God couldn't hear me. Or didn't want to. 'What's wrong with Him?'

I prayed softly, nonetheless, 'God, please, please save me! Save me from emptiness!'

THE NEXT DAY, we travelled with two policemen to Ras Ajdir. I got back only fifteen of my sixty dollars—the trip cost forty-five dollars for me and one of the policemen. The Africans had to pay for the other one as well as for the return journey of these two servants of the state.

They stamped 'Entry Ban' on my passport, loosened the fetters round my wrists and ordered me to 'Disappear!' I walked to the Libyan border post. The Africans were quicker and passed Libyan border control before me. I sat down between the two border posts. Looked to the left and to the right—into the twentieth and the eighteenth centuries. On both sides were a few pigeons. They were flying freely, now to the left, now to the right, wherever they wished. One always landed at the same place. Precisely where, on the left, the office was situated. There were children having fun too, travelling to the left or the right, with their families. The faces in the cars, both smiling and sad. I sat there for a long time. Thought about dancing and screaming but there were too many people. I got up and shuffled slowly over to the right, to the yellow desert that was supposed to be green.

'God—for fuck's sake—save me!'

BACK IN LIBYA, I heard no more from Abu-Agela. Later—several years and thousands of prayers later—I finally found a way, after all, to get into Turkey. The ship put to sea from the harbour in Tripoli and landed barely a week later in Izmir. For the first time in my life, I travelled by ship for seven days.

Up on deck, I lazed about with the other young men. The first few days, we stared at the vast Mediterranean. The last few days, we just waited, bored and desperate to reach the shore. There weren't even any women to flirt with. The few on board were accompanied by men and out of our reach. No opportunity to re-enact a film scene, to spend a romantic night with a seductive woman. The only woman travelling alone was a Russian. She enjoyed the best business of her entire life, for sure. While she spent the whole day horizontal in her cabin, the Libyan men queued up outside her door to do it with her. One night, I saw her smoking, up on deck. She was so worn out she could barely walk.

I met a nice Kurdish boy called Hewe. We spent a large part of the journey together. He'd been working in Libya and wanted to visit his family in northern Iraq. Or in 'Kurdistan', as he proudly called it. We chatted and he told me a lot, including how the Iraqi soldiers had killed his brother right before his eyes. 'That was 1991, in the resistance. The soldiers rounded up all the young men in our village, like cattle. Shot them all. In the end, only women, children and old men remained.'

Hewe had plans for later. 'I want to go to Germany. I have a friend there. He says the Germans offer Iraqis asylum.'

He fell silent for a while, then looked up at the sky with his blue eyes and murmured, 'I am a person who has nothing to do with politics. I just want to earn money in Germany and then return to Kurdistan when the situation has improved. I just want to live in peace with my mother and my sisters.'

After two days, the ship reached the harbour in Beirut. We were allowed to walk round the harbour area for a few hours but not beyond the walls. I looked out at Beirut—white houses, small mountains and countless posters. Not one of the president, though.

'Beautiful!' Hewe said, quickly interpreting my glances at the town. 'No pictures of the president—that can only be a good sign, right?'

An answer to this rhetorical question would have been superfluous. I continued to look at the town without a word. I'd heard a lot about it. War, literature and art, mourning, pretty women, murderers and homeless gods from other countries—like the artists and poets and singers and whores who, in the seventies, wrote their common history on the streets of this wonderful town. I thought for a moment about leaping over the harbour wall and staying in Beirut. It would have been easy. The wall was low and the police were busy with the ships and their passengers. In the end, I chose not to. I'd heard that you couldn't get a residence permit here without knowing someone in a political party. 'And that's not the right thing for me, is it?'

The ship sailed on. A few days later, we finally landed in Izmir. I didn't want to stay so I left that same day for Istanbul. At the bus station in Izmir, I said goodbye to

Hewe. 'The world is small, my friend!' he said, convinced we'd meet again.

We never did. That's how it goes. On such a long journey, you get to know not only people and towns and a new life but also the mysteries of the world's secret soundscape. Hewe, the Russian, her long queue could all well have been part of that soundscape.

IN ISTANBUL, I knew neither the language nor the people. I just had to look for the smugglers on Taksim Square, the European centre of Istanbul. No problem.

Taksim Square and its surroundings were quite magnificent, as was the square round the Republic Monument, populated by countless pigeons and street musicians. I looked for a spot on a bench every day—to watch the pigeons and the people and listen to the music. Not far away it was from the narrow streets where there was no dearth of brothels, and where, behind shop windows, the most seductive ladies displayed their charm. There, I should never have wanted to walk alone at night. Gay men, waiting for custom, lined the edge of the road. They spoke to every man who passed and were sometimes so persistent that I'd preferred a detour to being felt up by them. At first I'd thought them women but a second, closer look made me realize the truth. Their deep voices apart, they were actually very pretty, trim 'women'.

On Taksim Square, like all refugees, I had also to do with another kind of human being, the kind that certainly didn't show a feminine side—the people-smugglers. Prepared to do anything for money. Sometimes, I called them 'the extraterrestrials'. They had a special character, special qualities found in executioners, torturers, secret service agents and pimps.

One of them was called Azad. A Kurd from Sulaymaniyah in northern Iraq. Along with more than thirty refugees, he transported me by lorry to Edirne, a town near the border of Turkey and Greece. From there, after a two-hour march through the forests, we reached the Ebrus. He and his helpers fixed up a rubber dinghy to convey us to the opposite bank. Once we landed on the Greek side, we marched across the country for another four to five hours and finally set up camp in a valley.

Azad was squatting a little apart from the refugees. I sat behind a stone with a Kurd called Hama. The one family in our troop of refugees—a father, mother and little daughter—had found a place about fifty metres away. Most of the travellers fell asleep while Hama told me about his plans for life in Europe. 'I'll work, save up. Then fetch my fiancée from Kurdistan and marry her.'

He told me a lot, even about the history of Kurdistan, after 1991. 'We get out of one lot of shit and land in another. The Kurdish leaders have been fighting each other for years, all wanting to be the boss. They come to some arrangement for a while. Then they start fighting again. And it's us poor bastards that get screwed. We suffered under Saddam and now we suffer under our own people. What a crap fate!'

'There'll have to be a solution at some point!'

'At some point? In the next life, you mean!'

Suddenly, he looked up. 'Azad's still awake. And the woman in that family—look!'

We peeped out from behind our stone. She crept over to Azad and then crawled under his blanket, quietly. I watched her husband. He was lying on his stomach, his arm protectively round his daughter. His back was quivering, as if caressed by an icy wind. 'He's crying,' Hama whispered.

'But why is he letting her?'

'That's the price for the trip.'

'What?'

'One of Azad's aides mentioned that the husband has no money. That Azad took them along for free. The payment is a few nights with the wife.'

Now, God no doubt needs my help to save Him! I thought. Why's He not shifting His arse in Heaven? I felt a deep hatred against Him. That night, I felt the urge to kill someone rise in me. This feeling came upon me only rarely. And only in the case of certain people. I'd have liked most to tear the heart from the body of Azad, to barbecue it and serve it to the husband for dinner. Thereafter, on all such journeys, I carried a knife. On that journey, I even cherished the hope that the Greek police would track us down and arrest us. Then I could have turned Azad in. It was well known that smugglers, if caught, could expect especially harsh penalties. The police did indeed catch us and a significant part of the group was indeed arrested. But Azad managed to fuck off in time.

Every smuggler I've met always managed to fuck off in time. Hama believed that 'They can smell the police! They disappear so quietly and quickly, it's as if they'd never been there. No one knows how they do it.' Some refugees even said the smugglers had an agreement with the border police. If one group makes it to Athens unhindered, the next is for the police. That was why the smugglers always managed to get out in time. Who knows? In the forgotten border region between Turkey and Greece, nothing is impossible.

I spent a few days in jail, then the Greek police brought us back to the Turkish border. There, we were arrested by the Turkish police and put in jail again.

'God, save me from emptiness!'

I HAD THE FEELING that I'd never get out of Turkey. It was incredibly difficult to move round the border area between Greece and Turkey. Often, the police were lying in wait behind a hill or at the entrance to a valley. I was arrested several times and, again and again, spent days in a border police cell until I was freighted back by bus to Istanbul. Back then, there was an unwritten law about the destination of illegal refugees in Turkey. If you were arrested at the border, you were taken to Istanbul. But if you were arrested in Istanbul, you were deported to Iraq or Iran. So you had to keep your eyes especially open in Istanbul. There was always a way out. You could bribe a Turkish policeman with ten dollars.

I spent almost a week in the cell at the border. There was nothing to do but wait. Sometimes, the police took us to remote villages and made us clean the streets. Each time you ended up in a Turkish border prison, a policeman recorded your name. Then you were photographed and fingerprinted. Usually, a refugee never gives his real name. Each time he's arrested, he thinks of a new name. If he's found out, he could expect several months in jail. The Turkish police have a whole string of names for me, each with the same face and the same fingerprints.

Once, there were over a hundred of us, only Arabs and Iraqi Kurds. Sad, as if we were about to be sent to Hell. I decided to crack a joke—to make them smile for a moment, at least—and thought up a funny name for myself. Especially since I'd noticed that the policeman who was about to write down our names was the one who'd hit a few of us with great zeal when we'd been arrested. When he planted himself in front of me, in his ridiculous khaki rags and grinning like a child, and asked me for my name, I said, loudly and clearly, 'Ana Maniuk!' A while later, he came into our cell to send us for photographs and fingerprints. When he called my name—'Ana Maniuk'—I stayed quiet. 'Ana Maniuk,' he shouted again. Still I said nothing. The third time, he was louder and more impatient: 'Ana Maniuk!' The other prisoners were laughing so hard that tears rolled down their cheeks. Only the fourth time did I identify myself. In Arabic, 'ana maniuk' means 'I am an arsehole.'

AFTER SEVERAL FAILED ATTEMPTS to cross the Turkey–Greece border, I wanted to find work. An invalid passport, no residence permit and no knowledge of the language—it wasn't easy. I decided to go to Antakya, near the Turkey–Syria border. I'd heard that most people there spoke Arabic. They did, but that didn't help me in any way. I stayed for a day, then returned to Istanbul. Asked round in a great many shops and businesses. With no luck. In a cafe called al-Salam—peace—I ordered a glass of tea. I had no idea what to do next. The paths were blocked, the emptiness stinking to high heaven.

Then the big-bellied cafe owner came up to me. 'Heard you're looking for work?'

'Yes.'

'I've something for you.'

'What?'

'Not hard work. More like no work. You just have to marry a woman I know. You'll get a residence permit then. It'll be a sham marriage but you'd work with her.'

'What do you mean? Work as what?'

'You'd deal with the money and protect her. She'll be visited in the evenings by men who want some fun.'

'I'd be a pimp?'

'No, a lust facilitator!'

'What's the difference? Thanks, but no!'

I looked up into the bright sky. 'God, where on earth are you? Missing already?' I paid for my tea and left. Returned to Istanbul and again tried to flee to Greece.

Each time I was in the forests and mountains at the Turkey–Greece border, I felt the urge to write but didn't dare succumb to it for fear that the police might catch me. In Istanbul, it wasn't possible either for it is always full of people. And to write I need to be alone.

THE LAST, AND FINALLY SUCCESSFUL, ATTEMPT to reach Greece took almost a whole month. In the end, though, I got to Athens after all.

Greece was a cut above the countries I'd been in until then. In Athens, and on the western borders of the country, there was no need to be afraid of being deported back to Turkey. This no-fear made life a bit more bearable, though I had to fight against other difficulties. Here, too, I felt that unceasing emptiness. I didn't know what best to do. Moreover, an army of refugees from Iraq, Iran, Kurdistan, Pakistan, Afghanistan and Albania could be found all over the streets of Athens. Especially in the centre, at Omonia Square.

In the first few weeks, a child kept me busy—an Iraqi Kurd who'd lost his parents on the run. I spent two hours every day with him. He lived at Caritas in Athens and a few other refugees helped look after him. Sherzad was about a year old. He had been on the road with his parents and fifteen other refugees. He was already rather heavy for his age and his parents were delighted to have found obliging young men in the group willing to share the load. And so, the boy went from one shoulder to the next and had great fun despite the arduous walk. The group, though, was discovered by the Greek police. Some, including Sherzad's parents, were arrested. Sherzad himself escaped on the back of one of the young men and ended up with the rest of the group in Athens. His parents were taken back to Istanbul. Through the mysterious contacts of people-smugglers between Turkey and Greece, they got hold of the phone number of Caritas in Athens. The mother called almost every day and wept. Fortunately, about a month later, they managed to come to Athens. Their tears of joy burst all dams. The old Greek lady, who'd looked after Sherzad so lovingly for all that time, organized a reunion party. King for the day was Sherzad, of course.

Life in Athens wasn't as easy for me as it was for Sherzad. The child had found people willing to help him. Adults have to look out for themselves. And so I went off, in search of work. The only thing I found was the business of phone cards. I met Mohammed, who'd also fled from Iraq. He was trying to get to London—his uncle had been living there since the seventies. Mohammed was a communist—not a theory man, though, but a hands-on one. He always sided with the weak. Always dreamt of a better world. True, he had yet to hold a book in his hand but he liked people who were fond of reading. He also liked the communist idea but couldn't say why. What I liked in him was his love for people. He was willing to help anyone who needed help.

Mohammed got me the phone-card job. We teamed up, but it wasn't easy work. It was very dangerous, in fact, and meant a huge loss for the Greek economy. Mohammed borrowed from a Pakistani a so-called joker card that worked in every public phone and, what's more, recharged itself after every conversation. You could use up five hundred drachma on a call, then quickly remove and re-insert the card—and the five hundred drachma would be back on the card! The money earned in this way we had to split with the Pakistani. The Pakistanis in Greece were notorious for their technological tricks. Our customers were refugees for the most part and a few Greek down-and-outs who knew exactly where to find us. We used the phones round Omonia Square and in the Plaka, the area round the Acropolis. We sold five-hundred-drachma conversations for two hundred. The customers saved three hundred per call. The two hundred was our profit.

The only difficult thing was avoiding the *asfalias* —the security police in Athens. They were always out and about on their motorbikes and often came out of nowhere. That's why, as a matter of principle, we worked in pairs. One accompanied the customer, the other kept watch. One night—it was my turn to keep a lookout—a gigantic *asfali* (as we called them) turned up without my hearing or seeing the slightest thing. Quick as a flash, Mohammed dropped the joker card. The *asfali* arrested us and searched the ground carefully. When he found the joker card, though, he just tossed it away.

'Where are your drugs?'

He searched us but couldn't find anything. So he punched Mohammed in the face and gave me a mighty kick. 'Go . . .' he said, in English.

Relieved, and almost a little happy, we ran as fast as we could. Later, we came back, found the card and then went back home. Whooping and laughing cockily, we even did a few wild dance steps among the old Greek houses. Mohammed was acting like a child and burst into an old Iraqi folk song:

Fisherman! Can you catch me a sardine!
How odd, you a city boy, me a Bedouin.

The next day, Mohammed returned the card to the Pakistani and looked for another job. I decided to go to Patras. There, I had to wait for a long time before I could board the ship to Italy.

My paths in Italy were simple. I landed in Bari. I'd heard that getting from there to another European country wasn't a big problem. I didn't stay long in Bari and its narrow streets. After just an hour, I was determined to continue to Rome. So I went to the railway station. At a street corner, I saw two Kurds I knew from Patras. I went up to them and asked if they wanted to go to Rome too.

'Yes, but we're afraid. We can't speak English.'

'I can.'

'Will you buy our tickets for us?'

'Gladly, but will you pay for mine? I don't have much money on me—and I want to get to Rome too.'

They looked at each other. 'Okay!'

'Your trousers are dirty,' one of them said. 'That will draw attention. Don't you have any others?'

'No.'

'I do. Put them on.'

And so I travelled by train from Bari to Rome. The two Kurds thanked me and went into a different compartment. It was night. I fell into a deep and very calm sleep. Arrived in Rome early in the morning. Saw my friends there—the refugees at every corner and against every wall. Camping there, as if the main station were a bazaar. Some were selling bread-with-egg, tea or phone cards. Others were working as financial intermediaries. The Europe-based friends and acquaintances of a refugee transferred money to the intermediaries' account. They then paid out cash to the refugee. Not without taking the appropriate commission, of course. The people-smugglers also had their patches, though the demand for their services wasn't very great here. They worked, almost exclusively, for families that didn't have a clue or that wanted to reach their destination as quickly as possible.

Single men, who formed the largest part of the flow of refugees, organized their own onward journeys. Took a train to the border and continued from there alone.

On my first day in Rome, I met a Moroccan refugee who spent each night at the station. He showed me rectories, monasteries and other church institutions where I could have a shower and sometimes get food and pocket money. I stayed in Rome for a few weeks. I didn't need much money there and I could move about freely.

I enjoyed my time there a lot—the broad streets, the old houses, the beautiful women. I strolled from one square to the next, then returned to the station. Walked through the town centre, looking at the old stones.

It rained one day and I felt an incredible desire to dance. Not because I was sad. No, not at all. Because I wanted to. And so I closed my eyes and danced. When I opened them again, I saw other people dancing round me. I stopped and began to applaud. I then went off, recalling Abba and Abd, the first people to dance with me in Baghdad. Abba wanted to be a philosopher, Abd a sociologist. We'd always wanted to dance in the rain in Rome. Why Rome? I don't know. Each time things went badly for us or it was raining and the streets of Baghdad emptied, we'd head for al-Sade and dance. 'Like Zorba the Greek!' Abba would shout. 'It's as if we were in Rome!' Abd would shout. We would dance until the rain dried up or our tears did. Abba and Abd stayed in Baghdad. Abba became a famous document forger and, later, the bodyguard of an Islamic leader. Abd a prison warder.

I, though, danced in the rain in Rome. A refugee. A pigeon, lost and homeless.

The refugees at the main station told me that I had to go to the police and get a refugee ID that was valid for a fortnight. Within that fortnight, the refugee had to leave Italy. To get the ID, you had to spend a night at the police station. So I set out to look for the nicest central police station. I reached just as dusk was about to fall. The policemen fingerprinted and photographed me, then took me to a cell. They left the door open, though. I was the only prisoner. Finally, I could sleep in a clean room. In the days before, I'd either slept in the station building or in a tunnel with the homeless and the refugees.

That night, in my comfortable cell, I couldn't sleep a wink. The guards were making a hellish noise with their night-time gambling and boozing. They got so drunk that one of them even came to my cell to take me with him. He found a chair for me, got me a bottle of beer and pressed a few cards into my hand. I hardly knew a word of Italian. And they had no Arabic. Their English, too, was so bad that it was no help at all. Nonetheless, we chatted all night and had a great time, laughing and roaring. I even began telling them something in Arabic. They laughed and laughed. We drank and danced as if we were somewhere else, not in a police station. By dawn, by about four maybe, we had totally lost control. No one knew what was going on.

Next morning, the men on the next shift arrived, gave me my ID and said in English, 'Go!'

In Rome, I got a ticket and travelled to Bolzano, on the border between Italy and Austria. I spent a few days there, sleeping at the station, going to Caritas to eat and strolling through the town centre, watching the people shopping, talking, kissing . . . Then, hidden in a train, I travelled one night to Germany and ended up in Munich. I didn't want to stay there for long, though. The refugees at the main station in Rome had shared an interesting classification of the European countries. Britain, they said, was good for intellectuals as it had many different Arabic or Kurd newspapers, magazines, TV and radio channels and organizations. Sweden, they said, supported families, students and, again, intellectuals. Germany, on the other hand, was suitable for workers and people who wanted to save money. Germany was one big factory. Life in one big factory wasn't for me. It was therefore my intention to travel through Germany and on, until Sweden. My journey was brought to a halt, though—by the German police.

'I want to go to Sweden,' the interpreter translated for me.

'Why?' the police official asked.

'I want to go to Sweden.'

'You're here, illegally. You can't continue to Sweden. I'm arresting you! Don't you understand?'

'I want to go to Sweden.'

'You can apply for asylum, but only for here.'

'I want to go to Sweden.'

'We now have your fingerprints. They'll be forwarded to all countries offering asylum. If you try to flee, you'll be brought back to Germany.'

I was very sad at not being able to reach Sweden. What could I do, other than submit to my fate?

This, then, was where my journey ended. Truth be told, it didn't end at all. It only took on new forms. The German authorities sent me from one asylum seekers' home to the next. The first few days, I spent in a home near Ansbach, then in Bayreuth and then in Passau. When I'd finally been given a residence permit, I went to Munich. I wanted to look for work, to save up for a language course. For months, I ran from one authority to the next, seeking support. No luck. And it was almost impossible to finance that kind of thing from my own pocket—Munich's an extremely expensive town.

Things were generally difficult in Germany, in this one big factory. I did some work as a cleaner and a labourer for a large number of agencies. It took me a while to begin to learn the language. I worked in the mornings, attended a course in the afternoons. My life was full of appointments and commitments. Yet that never-ending emptiness began to spread through me again. I tried everything possible—and impossible—to get my life back together but foundered, often, on the numerous paragraphs and bureaucratic rules under which Germany is buried. To me, this country was like a town hidden behind a wall. If you want in, you have to make a hole in the wall. The wall, though, is made of iron. It can take years to make that hole. And what do you find in the end?

Again and again, I tried to make a new beginning—inside the hole, in the wall or behind it, but . . . The emptiness in this country's forests and mountains was just as great and powerful as the one I'd encountered in the desert. I was gradually seeing how great and powerful the emptiness is that you may encounter wherever you go. It is so great and powerful, it takes away the air I breathe. My prayer came back to mind but for some reason I didn't want to say it. And yet I haven't forgotten my last great wish—to be granted asylum on some other planet. And, perhaps, to find my great-uncle Jabar there . . .

SIX
The Miracles

I SWEAR ON ALL CREATURES, both visible and invisible that I have nine lives. Like a cat. No, no, twice as many. Cats would go green with envy. Miracles happen—in my life—always at the last minute. I believe in miracles. In those strange moments for which there is no other term. One of life's secrets, as it were. These miracles have much in common with coincidences. But I can't call them coincidences because a coincidence doesn't happen many times over. A coincidence is just a coincidence, as lame as that might sound. You can talk about one big coincidence in life, two at most, but not more. So there are events that are miracles, not coincidences—that's how I will put it, even if the logic isn't exactly Aristotelian. I'm not a superstitious person, the supernatural and subterrestrial are not for me. In the course of my life I've developed, so to speak, my own religious persuasion, one made to measure for me. Absolutely individual. To this day, for instance, I worship tyres. Yes, car tyres! To me they're not just a car's feet but guardian angels. I know that doesn't sound particularly intelligent, given that many people have lost their lives to car tyres. But car tyres can also *save* lives. And that is how the first miracle happened.

I was in jail in Baghdad. Being in jail in Baghdad is no miracle. In the nineties, it was even the norm. One day, we were taken on an unexpected journey. A never-to-be-forgotten journey. The guards got all the prisoners together, bound their hands, blindfolded them with bits of black cloth and put them in several cars. The cars moved slowly. Everything was dark. I could hear only my fellow prisoners breathing and my heart thumping. Could smell only the others' sweat and their old, damp clothes. After what seemed like half an eternity, an endless babble of voices reached my ears as did the roar of engines. I could hear the everyday noises of my home town again. The yells of children, the loud music from the music shops and the street dealers shouting: 'Fresh tomatoes, salad, fruits and vegetables, all fresh . . .' After a while, I could hear only the wind against the sides of the car. Then a sudden bang. The car stopped. The prison guards' voices drew closer. The door opened slowly and we heard the order, 'Out!' I moved, in slow motion, in order not to fall. 'Sit! On the ground!' I sucked in the air. It was cold but fresh. I knew this air. We were in the desert. But why?

The guards were talking to each other.

'We need to change the damn tyre as quickly as possible. Then catch up with the others.'

'That's impossible. We don't have a spare. We'll have to fix it!'

'How long will that take?'

'Half an hour, maybe!'

'Shit! They'll kill us. Get on with it.'

For half an hour, there was a deathly hush. The guards spoke little. Then, 'Get up and get in. Quick!' The car began to move but suddenly stopped again. Incomprehensible sounds from outside. A minute later, we drove off again. For a while I could hear the strong desert wind, then human voices and the sounds of countless cars. Perhaps we were back in town again. A few minutes later, the car stopped again. Again, the prison guards' voices drew closer. Again, the door opened. Again, we heard the order, 'Out!' I recognized the strange smell of the prison, the smell of damp, the smell of the sagging flesh of imprisoned people. Was it the same prison? Had it just been an outing?

The guards removed our bonds. I was back to the large section of our prison. Only twenty of us now. Where were the others? There'd been so many before. Three hundred, almost.

No one knew.

That evening, a guard came and gaped at us, surprised. 'Do you realize God loves you?'

'Why?'

'You're still alive!'

'What! Does that mean the others—?'

'Yes, they were executed in the desert. That car tyre saved you.'

I SWEAR ON ALL CAR TYRES—the next miracle followed soon after. In Iraqi slang, we refer to jail as 'behind the sun'. It was clear to me that I'd never be allowed back to life on this side of the sun. Walking from the dark side back into the brightness of lightbulbs I began to consider impossible. Yet the day came when the government declared an amnesty for all political prisoners. Because I'd been charged with minor and insignificant crimes, I was permitted, with all the other minor and insignificant prisoners, to see the light of the sun again. The major and significant prisoners had all been executed long ago. I waited for a month to be released. It was a very long month, longer than a decade! Eventually, though, I was 'in front of the sun' again. I got into a taxi. A short time later, I was home. I knocked. My mother's face appeared.

'Yes?'

'Good afternoon!'

'Good afternoon!'

'How are you today?'

'Fine, and you?'

'Fine. Don't you recognize me?'

'No, who are you? Is it one of the boys you want?'

'Do you really not recognize me?'

'No!'

'It's Rasul.'

She stared at me, speechless, drew her breath in sharply and fell unconscious to the floor. She couldn't have recognized me! How was she to? A good eighty-five kilos and burnt brown when I left, I'd returned fifty-five kilos and as pale as a piece of Gouda. Eighteen months of hardly any bread and no sun at all had changed me beyond recognition.

I SWEAR ON THE AMNESTY—this miracle needed another miracle in order to really save me. The miracle of the chance to flee Iraq. As expected, the gods and devils of the government wanted me behind bars again—or, better still, hanging from the ceiling. They sent me an official letter, demanding that I end my studies and report to the army. I was also to report to the security police. I decided to flee. I had no desire whatsoever to go 'behind the sun' again.

I left our part of town and went into hiding with relatives. There were so many policemen in the streets, you'd have thought they were a people in their own right. But thanks to my friend Abba, I could still be out and about. For the next few months, he supplied me with fake ID more than fifteen times, with just as many names and professions. Each time, I had to learn by heart my new name and all the details that went with it. Even today, I wonder which one of them I really was. And who they all were.

The day finally came when I could leave all those names behind and sail the seas, using my real name. Getting a passport in Iraq wasn't easy but I managed. Two official documents were required—one confirming you'd done your military service, the other that you weren't subject to a travel ban. The whole thing cost a million Iraqi dinars, or a thousand American dollars. Even with the best will in the world, I couldn't meet all three requirements. Of course, I hadn't reported to the army. Of course, I was subject to a travel ban. And, of course, I didn't have a million dinars to spare.

An acquaintance of my elder brother worked as a policeman and wasn't short of contacts with various Baghdad authorities. He offered to alter the data the authorities held on me and to arrange a passport that would enable me to flee to Jordan. He would need two thousand dollars from me, though. Two thousand dollars! Where would I get that kind of money? This time, it was the women in the family who saved me. My sisters sold their jewellery and my mother sold her brother her part of their father's house. Though my family had barely enough to live on, I managed to get the money together.

Within a week, the policeman managed to alter my data. Eighteen months in jail for political reasons became eighteen months of military service, and a drifter, about to abscond, became an art-college student. Finally, I had a passport with my real name. Even the travel ban vanished from the records for forty-eight hours, giving me two days to leave the country for Jordan. Once all the bribes were paid, precisely thirty dollars remained. The policeman returned them to me—a gesture, to help get me started.

I said goodbye to my family and boarded the bus. It crossed the Iraqi border and continued towards Amman. Even now, I can't believe I managed to leave Iraq. Years later, I still have dreams about the Iraqi police arresting me at the border and I begging them, in tears, to release me.

On the other side of the world, in Jordan, two men in uniform suddenly boarded the bus. Sat down behind me. Oh God, no! What do they want me for? They're armed. Should I get off the bus, make a run for it? They're just Jordanian soldiers. But soldiers are soldiers. Maybe the Iraqi government has put them on to me!

With these, and similar thoughts, I passed the many long hours until we arrived in Amman. I took my bag, got off the bus and ran. Like a world champion. After a while, I stopped—I was sweating—and turned round. No one. The people in the street stared at me as if I wasn't quite right in the head. An old man, standing outside his food shop, beckoned me over. 'What's wrong, my son? Why are you running like that?'

'Nothing!'

'Where are you from?'

'Iraq.'

'I see. Come, drink some water.'

He gave me a glass of water and a pat on the shoulder.

'Don't worry. This is not Iraq but Jordan.'

I SWEAR ON ALL FAKE DOCUMENTS—I didn't plan these miracles. They always just happened, at the end of long cruel periods.

When I landed in Africa, I lived there for years without a single miracle. All my attempts to cross the Mediterranean failed. I took on all kinds of jobs, just to survive, until the day I met Miriam. I can still remember her scent. The smell of the sea in the evening. She was in her early twenties, perhaps, a round white face and red lips, as if it was chilli she'd used, not lipstick. We first met in the Grand Tourist Hotel on Omar al-Mukhtar Street in Tripoli. She worked as a chambermaid. Every morning, she'd come into my room, empty the bin, say 'Hello' and 'Welcome to the Grand Tourist Hotel!' Then smile and leave. Was she mad? This hotel had nothing to do with tourists. An old building, six or seven floors. Full of foreigners, gays, whores, alcoholics, dealers and criminals. And filth. And a toilet in the corridor, fit for everything but going to the toilet.

Miriam was both a chambermaid and a whore. I paid her for the first night. Told her I just wanted to talk, not fuck.

'How come?' she asked, surprised.

'I've never paid for sex.'

We did sleep together, all the same, that night. The second night she gave me my money back. Suddenly, it was something like love—like many of those strange feelings you don't expect and can't understand. I was with her for a month. She even wanted to pay for my hotel as I didn't have much money left. Though it cost only a dollar per night, I couldn't afford it. 'With the others, I'm doing my job,' she explained. 'But with you it's because I want to.'

She never would tell me why she sold her body. All she told me was that she was from Morocco and had been working in the hotel for the last two years. The hotel belonged to a police commander, also well known in Tripoli as a pimp. 'Policeman or pimp—there's not much of a difference here,' she said with a shrug.

She had to give her pimp a percentage of her earnings. 'There're some things you're better off not knowing. They can be very dangerous. You can be sure, though, that behind every whore and every nun, there's a sad story.'

I was trying to find work again but could only find odd jobs on building sites. My Iraqi passport was causing me concern too—it was valid for only another month. Having it extended at the Iraqi embassy wasn't an option. I knew what to expect there. A few difficult and worrying weeks followed. The Libyan police could deport me to Egypt at any time. The Egyptians would then deport me to Jordan. And the Jordanians to Iraq.

But then came the night that changed everything.

I was walking along the beach one evening, watching the boats and ships before returning to Omar al-Mukhtar Street to get something to eat. I crossed Green Square and continued towards a falafel stand. Suddenly, five men blocked my path. I couldn't see their faces. They beat me until I was lying on the ground, motionless. What was this all about? What was happening? I had no idea until one of them hissed, 'Fucking Iraqi! You're dead if we ever see you with Miriam again.'

I lay there, looked at the sky, the stars and couldn't hold back my tears. I got up again, with difficulty, and tried to return to the hotel. My body ached. I dragged myself through the masses of rubbish left behind by the street sellers. Outside the hotel was a man with my bag. He threw it at my feet and vanished behind the door. I took the bag and went back to the beach, laid it on the ground like a pillow and fell asleep.

Nightmares—never-ending—tormented me. Suddenly I saw Miriam's face. It wasn't a dream. The sun was shining, and Miriam took my hand. We got into a car. The driver didn't look like an Arab. She didn't say a word to me, Miriam. Instead, she kissed me the whole time. The driver was Turkish, I learnt later. He dropped us outside a flat in the town centre. Miriam took my passport and gave it to him. He promised to come back as quickly as possible. Miriam fetched a damp cloth and began cleaning my wounds. When she was done, she took her L&M cigarettes from her bag and put the packet on the table in front of me. She then went into the kitchen to make some tea. Tea in hand, she told me that the Turkish driver was arranging a visa for Turkey for me.

'How? It's impossible! My passport expires soon, and the Turks won't give an Iraqi a visa just like that!'

'You don't need to know the details. But you're off to Turkey today.'

'What about you? Won't you come with me?'

'I can't. It's my fate to stay here.'

'But if you can arrange a visa for me, you must be able to get one for yourself too.'

'You're like a child. You don't understand the world out there.'

I had some tea and smoked a cigarette, then we lay down and I fell asleep. When I woke up, I could hear Miriam. 'So tell me—'

'I have the visa and the ticket,' the Turk said. 'The ship sails at four this afternoon.'

Miriam looked at the clock on the wall. 'We have two hours.'

I boarded the ship. Miriam stood on the harbour. Waved goodbye with one hand, wiped her tears with the other.

I've not heard from Miriam since. I sent her six letters in the space of a year. Posted to the hotel address. But there was no reply.

I SWEAR ON MIRIAM'S LIFE—sometimes, I can hardly believe what I'm writing. The things that happened next don't happen even in fairy tales. In Istanbul, for instance. I was sitting with twenty Kurds in a top-floor, two-room apartment. Thirty square metres, barely. With us was Ahmed, a Turk from Iraq. He was very handsome and dreamt of going to Germany and becoming a great painter there. The flat belonged to our people-smuggler, who was to get us to Greece soon. The smuggler had run into me on Taksim Square. He came straight up to me and asked, 'Greece?'

'What?'

'Iraqi, Iranian, Pakistani or Afghan?—Greece?'

'Iraqi.'

'Me too but I'm a Kurd.'

'Great!'

'Car or foot?'

'What's the difference?'

'Foot, twenty days and five hundred dollars. Car, two days and fifteen hundred dollars.'

'On foot, please.'

'Come.'

People-smugglers know their clientele very well. A refugee doesn't behave like a normal person when he's out and about. He thinks everyone is a policeman. He's suspicious of everyone. He's not interested in shop windows or posters or women. He watches only people's faces, his eyes wander restlessly. Like a clock that has gone mad. He keeps looking over his shoulder, fear written on his face. In my case, the symptoms were probably very evident. I later learnt that many people-smugglers have this ability—it's known as their seventh sense.

None of my flatmates had a passport. All of them had left Iraq and entered Turkey illegally. My passport had now also expired and was useless. That meant all of us always had to stay indoors to avoid getting caught by the Turkish police. There was a clear agreement—the door was only to be opened after three knocks. One afternoon, though, someone hammered it five or six times. We all stood there, paralysed. Fear had completely demoralized me. Being deported to Iraq and landing in the hands of the Iraqi police again—that's all I could think of. Suddenly, the door was kicked in and three policemen rushed in. Shouting wildly, they forced us against the wall. A fat policeman with a mole on his nose kicked a Kurd in the stomach. The man fell to the floor and began to vomit. During which time I suddenly spotted the open window that led from our small room onto the terrace of the next building. The other two policemen were trying to get the Kurd back on his feet. The one with the mole was watching. Propelling myself off the wall, I raced to the window and jumped out. I could hear shouting behind me. Someone following. The buildings were high, about ten floors. I ran and ran. And heard women, down on the street and on the terraces across the way, shouting '*Hırsız, hırsız, hırsız!*'—Thief, thief, thief!

I reached the fifth building. There was now a side street between me and the next set of houses. I had no chance! I stopped and turned round. Behind me was Ahmed. And behind him, one of the policemen watching us through the window. The terrace of the final building had no door. I looked down. Three floors below there was another. I looked to the left and to the right. Pipes, only. And several windowsills. I jumped and landed with one foot on the gutter. Then hopped onto a windowsill. Ahmed was right behind me. The windowsill gave way beneath our weight. We plummeted onto the terrace. By the time I picked myself up, Ahmed was already at the door to the building. It was locked—damn! We looked at each other, helplessly.

'Fucking shit.'

Suddenly, we heard a voice, an old man. '*Gelmek*!'—Come! He was leaning out of a window. He waved us over, signalled that we should climb in through the window. Ahmed climbed in first. The man offered us a seat and began to question us. Ahmed spoke good Turkish, like all Iraqi Turkmens. He translated for me. Once we'd made it clear we weren't thieves but Iraqis trying to get to Greece, the man asked, 'Are you Shi'ites?'

'I'm not,' said Ahmed, 'but my friend Rasul is.'

The old man smiled. 'My name's Ali and I'm an Alevi. We Alevis are very like the Shi'ites. The Turkish government makes our life hell too.'

He got up, offered me his hand, then hugged and kissed me, calling me 'Brother Rasul'.

He gave us food and drink and talked to Ahmed about Iraq. From time to time, Ahmed would ask me something or translate a certain bit for me. About two hours later, Ali said he'd go down to the street and see if the police were still there. A few minutes later, he was back again. 'The air is clear, not a policeman to be seen.'

The old man said we could spend the night there but we decided to leave. We thanked him warmly and took our leave. I never saw Ali again.

Ahmed knew other people-smugglers. He found a Kurd for me, a Turkmen for himself. I ran into him again, later, on Omonia Square in Athens. He didn't recognize me. He was standing next to a smuggler, one with several thuggish bodyguards. I greeted Ahmed. He looked at me. But his blue eyes seemed lost, failed to focus. Each had a huge black circle at the centre. He wasn't as handsome as he had been in Turkey. Looked semi-derelict. Some refugees told me he'd become this smuggler's sex slave. 'Your man's got Ahmed hooked on drugs. Ahmed has to accompany him everywhere—as his "wife."'

I SWEAR ON ALI and all the Alevis—I didn't want to have to count on any more miracles. Of course not—what kind of fate would that be? But I had no choice. The next miracle hit me completely unexpectedly too. This time, I was with a smuggler and twenty-three refugees and already on the Greek side of the Ebrus. We'd been walking for almost three weeks, from the Turkish border near Edirne, past Komotini, to Xanthi, our final stop. During the day, we slept in the forest or in the mountains. From six in the evening until five in the morning, we walked, or ran. Along hidden paths through Greece. From Xanthi, it was impossible to walk any further. As the smuggler explained, there were only impassable mountains or the sea. We had to wait for a lorry to take us to Thessaloniki or Athens. We camped for a week behind a hill, near an old, deserted factory. Round us were small fields and dusty earth. The lorry didn't come. The bandits did instead. Late afternoon, just before sunset. We heard nothing but the shots. The smuggler jumped up. Six of us fled with him. Ran as fast as we could, without stopping to look. But we heard the bullets whistle past, on either side. I fell several times but picked myself up and ran on. We headed straight for the factory, hid inside. No one followed us.

The smuggler peered at me.

'Are you injured?'

'What?'

'Fuck, you're bleeding! They got you.'

I hadn't noticed, nor could I feel any pain. But I had been hit—twice. One bullet through my right hand. The other deep in my left calf.

The smuggler examined me more closely. 'These aren't real bullets. They're for animals. That means those guys weren't policemen!'

We waited another two hours before returning to our camp. That's what all smugglers did—after two or three hours, they went back to the starting point. When we arrived, our whole group was already there. They told us the men wanted money. And they got it. There were seven of them, all armed and masked. No one knew if they were policemen or bandits. The smuggler decided to stay with us and sleep here. He hoped to find a solution the next day. That night, though, my leg began to hurt. An intense throbbing pain. In the morning, the smuggler turned to me, 'You'll have to travel on your own by train. It will take the lorries another three to five days to arrive. And you won't last that long. Three days from now, at the latest, you'll be dead. I'll buy you a ticket. You can take the train to Athens. If you make it there, you'll be saved. You'll also be saved if the police arrest you—they'll make sure you get to a hospital.'

I agreed. A Kurd called Imad said he'd had enough and wanted to accompany me. Shortly after midday, our smuggler arrived with a car driven by a Greek. The smuggler gave us tickets and said the Greek would take us to the station.

We shaved and put on the clean clothes that every refugee has in his rucksack for such occasions. Then we got into the car. The Greek didn't say a word. Drove us through a small town before stopping outside a low building with a sign that read, 'Xanthi Station'. He went off right away. Two minutes later, he was back—to accompany us to the platform. Five minutes later, we boarded the train and he said goodbye with a curt, '*Yassu*!'

The train pulled off. After a while, the ticket inspector came to check our tickets.

'Passport.'

'No.'

He took us right up to the front of the train, near the engine, and tried to tell us to wait there for him. He went into the driver's cab and reached for the phone. Imad and I looked at each other but said nothing. Of course, we knew what this meant for us. The train began to slow down. Not far off, there seemed to be a small town. The ticket inspector came back out of the driver's compartment and passed us on his way to the middle of the train. The train stopped, the doors opened and passengers got off. Imad looked at me and whispered, 'No police!' We jumped out of the train and ran down the street. It was dark. No one followed us.

We ran towards a big park. Lots of people were sitting around, eating or chatting.

'Man, that was just like an action film!' Imad grinned.

'You're right—one based on a true story.'

Fortunately, I was in no pain at all. You wouldn't have thought there was a bullet in my body. In the park, we spent our time watching people in the street, marvelling at the gorgeous Greek women. Time was passing quickly and we didn't really know what to do with ourselves. I spoke to a young lad. He had a beer and some peanuts on the ground beside him.

'Hello, can you help me?' I asked in English. 'I'd like a ticket to Athens. I have money. Will you buy it for me?'

Where we were, exactly—the name of the town—interested us very little, if at all, at this point. I'd always thought it was Kavala. Kavala, though, has no trains and, so, no station, as I'd learn years later. We were, in fact, in Drama. A more appropriate name you couldn't have asked for, given our predicament.

My English was nothing special but the young Greek's English was no better. He nonetheless gave the impression that he was enjoying our conversation. And so, it seemed that our tragic drama in Drama had been resolved. I told the Greek we were Iraqis and didn't want to buy the tickets ourselves. He took us to a small park outside the station. Then went into the station alone. A short while later, he returned to explain that a ticket to Athens cost twenty dollars and the train left at one in the morning. Imad gave him fifty. The boy bought the tickets. He'd changed the rest of the dollars into drachma. Imad said he could keep it. He looked at us, smiled and put the money in his pocket. Finally, he pointed at the clock above the main entrance. 'You have only thirty minutes.' He took his leave and we thanked him.

We waited. It was a very long half hour. Imad thought every person round the station was a policeman. I tried to calm him, though I had the same feeling. He, however, swore—on all his prophets—that they all looked like policemen. We moved slowly in the direction of the station concourse. Just before we got there, a bus stopped at the entrance and a group of Africans accompanied by two blond Greeks got out. In no time at all, the station was reverberating with the sounds of a Turkish bazaar. Happy 'Hello Africa'-s were being shouted everywhere. I quickly grabbed Imad by the arm and, as casually as possible, we got in among the Africans and boarded the train—without being stopped. Imad thought it better if, on the train, we separated. 'If one of us is arrested, they might not look for the other one.'

So he turned right and I turned left. I sat down opposite an old lady. About seventy and very like my grandmother, who had died while I was in jail in Baghdad. I even thought I could see my grandmother's smile on her face. I leant back on the headrest and closed my eyes.

Suddenly, I felt a soft hand on mine. Startled, I opened my eyes. The old lady was leaning over me, looking at me, worried and a little apprehensive. She was examining my wound, which had become inflamed during the day and was now pretty bad. She spoke to me in Greek. I answered, simply, 'I am from Iraq.'

She knew only a few words of English. She said, 'Ticket?'

I held it out and she took it from me. She whispered a soothing 'Okay!' and tried to gesture to me what she wanted to say. 'Have a good sleep. I'll deal with everything else.'

I think the word 'Iraq' was enough for her to understand my situation. She was my guardian angel for the rest of the journey. When the tickets were inspected, she showed ours together, and I'm almost certain she told the ticket inspector that I was with her. She bought me cheese, bread and a Coke. I slept like a baby. I woke up, briefly, a few times, but went straight back to sleep and slept until the next day when we arrived in Athens. She then took me to the Red Cross, where—with a friendly 'Bye-bye!'—she left me in the care of a nurse.

Whether this old lady was a Greek goddess in my delirium or a reality, I don't quite know. I only remember how, in the train, I suddenly felt severe pain, pain I had barely been aware of with all the stress of the escape. That's probably why I didn't register everything clearly, but the tender face of the old lady has remained with me. I don't have any idea where Imad ended up. The doctor at the Red Cross told me, 'It's a miracle you're alive.'

I SWEAR ON THE OLD GREEK GODDESS—I can hate the world and, at the same time, love it. And with people, it's just the same. Always, there were murderers and rescuers, haters and lovers. I decided early on, though, to take the world as it is. I know a miracle always occurs at some point in my life. And that's some comfort, in this world of ours. The next small miracle happened soon. A few days before New Year's Eve. In Patras. This small, unassuming town had a beautiful, big harbour from which many ships set sail for Italy. There were refugees all over Patras, in old houses, in old factories, in the park. I camped with them for weeks. Word had it that the police wouldn't be operating strict checks between

Christmas and New Year. Entire groups of refugees were disappearing, on a daily basis. I'd had only bad luck, been arrested four times by the heavy-duty harbour police. Each time I'd been kicked out of the area. Each time by a policeman with an even harder kick.

On 29 December, I was gloomily strolling along the harbour wall and wistfully watching the departing lorries, ships and foot passengers. Dusk had already fallen. Suddenly, a storm broke. There was rain. Suddenly, the harbour was empty. A lorry without a tarpaulin was parked right beside a big ship that was ready to sail. Instinctively, I climbed the wall, dropped down on the other side, ran straight to the lorry and hid at the back of the hold. I found a large, black plastic sheet, threw it over me and lay beneath it, absolutely still. About ten minutes later, the rain stopped. I heard the driver climb in. He started the engine and drove straight onto the ship. Another twenty minutes later, the ship began to move.

A good while passed before I could hear no voices any more. I looked round the cargo deck. There were so many lorries, I was spoilt for choice. I decided, for reasons of safety, to look for a different one. Found a white one, with 'Italy' on the door. Why not? I unpacked my refugee kit—a small razor blade, a roll of Sellotape and a plastic bag. I made a cut with the blade down the tarpaulin and climbed through it, into the lorry. Inside, cardboard boxes were piled up to the roof. I managed to find a good place to lie down. Now, the Sellotape was called into action—to close the slit again, from the inside. I used the plastic bag to pee in.

For the entire journey, I heard nothing but the whistle of the wind, the roar of the waves and the lorries creaking as they rocked with the ship. The crossing was very long. I had to lie where I was, the whole time, and not move. Finally, the ship docked. The lorry set off. More than twenty minutes later, it stopped again. The driver got out and slammed the door. I waited another five minutes, peeled off the Sellotape, cautiously put my head out and looked round. The sky was dark. I looked down. I was in a harbour. Some harbour, somewhere. It was definitely European though, I realized right away. Everything written on the lorries and posters was in Roman script. Hardly anyone was round.

I jumped down and walked towards the fence. It was very high. Beyond it was a brightly lit street, with lots of people. I'd always heard from smugglers that, in Italy, refugees could do whatever they liked, except get arrested within a harbour area. If you were arrested in the harbour area, you were deported immediately. To Turkey, or some other place. If you were arrested outside the harbour area, you were allowed to stay, Italy being a country of asylum.

And so I ran the last bit like a horse straight up to the fence and, like an Olympian athlete, hurled myself—don't ask me how—with a great leap over to the other side. I looked back but didn't see anything unusual. I tried to keep walking, as casually as possible. How I managed that daring leap is beyond me. But, as is well known, fear can give you incredible strength, if not a pair of wings.

Once on the well-lit street, I asked my way to the station and trains to Rome. I was now sure I was in Italy. You could hardly miss the pizza shops. Which town it was exactly didn't interest me. My one concern was the next train to Rome. In the large station, I bought a ticket and travelled to the capital that same night. There were no police or annoying ticket inspectors. A long time later, I found out that I'd landed in Bari harbour. Early in the morning, I reached Rome, where I'd barely left the main station when I happened upon my friends for ever—refugees. They'd made themselves at home in every corner of the huge Termini station.

At about nine in the evening, I joined a crowd of people who led me straight to a big building on a huge square. A man was delivering a speech and, judging by the applause, was a prominent figure. The pope? Several years and just as many New Year's Eves later, I learnt where I'd actually celebrated my first New Year's Eve on European soil. It was the Victor Emmanuel Monument, or the 'typewriter', as it's ironically known by the inhabitants of that impressive metropolis.

I SWEAR ON RAIN, and on New Year's Eve—I didn't want any more miracles. I'd had enough, I just wanted some peace. Despite that, another tiny miracle came my way.

I'd ended up in Germany by now—Bayreuth, to be precise—in a home for asylum seekers. The judges and my interpreter had listened to my whole story. They said they could only grant me asylum if I could prove I'd been a political prisoner in Iraq. Evidence, yet again! How the hell was I going to do that? Which Iraqi torturer was going to be so kind as to confirm in writing that he'd beaten me to death, nearly, or done who knows what to me? Then, luckily, I recalled a day in jail when we'd been visited by the members of a European organization. After the Second Gulf War, the United Nations had demanded that the Iraqi government allow a few international organizations to inspect Iraqi authorities and jails and write a report. These organizations had drawn up lists of prisoners' names, a measure I'd dismissed back then as stupid and pointless. I did, however, think it appropriate to tell the female judge about it. She promised to make inquiries at Amnesty International. A few weeks later, I was visited by my interpreter. He grinned triumphantly and looked at me as if I was a hero. 'Hell! They found your name.'

I SWEAR ON AMNESTY INTERNATIONAL—I've often wondered how on earth I'm still alive. Why did all these miracles happen to me? Why, of all people, me? I don't think there's an answer to questions like that. But that's how I ended up with my own, personal saints—Amnesty International, the rain, New Year, the Red Cross, the old Greek goddess, Ali and the Alevis, Miriam, fake documents, my mother and my sisters, the amnesty and, last but not least, car tyres. They're all of comfort to me in the severe weather the world sometimes experiences.

SEVEN

On the Wings of the Raven

Many cultures fear the raven. It is regarded as a bird of ill, a bringer of bad luck. I was often that kind of unlucky raven for people. Wherever I went, ill fortune wasn't slow to follow. Without wishing to, I often brought nothing but grief and misery upon my fellow humans. That was my fate, my very personal fate.

It began in Baghdad. When I began primary school, Saddam Hussein came to power. I failed at school and the teachers called me 'the stupid one'. Saddam failed to rule and his stupidities transformed the country into a hell. I can easily imagine that all the wars and disasters that have happened in Iraq since I was born have happened only because of me. Iraq was nothing but a ruin when I left it behind. I was its unlucky raven from the very beginning. I was able to observe this later too. Again and again, when I stayed in other countries. I was—and am—convinced of that. Completely convinced.

The unlucky raven in me destroyed the lives of many people. It was I who devastated many countries on earth. Yes, I. Too many disasters and corpses lined my way for me to think otherwise. I tried again and again not to believe this, but fate would have it no other way. The same game was repeated over and over. Barely had I set foot in the Jordanian capital of Amman when the Bread Revolution broke out. In no time at all, I had wreaked havoc in Jordan with my black bird. The Jordanian government had increased the price of bread and so the poor people in the south had taken to the streets to vent their displeasure. So far, not so bad. What was bad was the subsequent counterinsurgency, using weapons and violence. People talked of many victims.

A month later, I wished to visit the small town of al-Karak where the Bread Revolution had begun. The police, though, wouldn't let the bus pass. They said only soldiers could go in and out of the town. Through the bus window, I could see nothing but ruins. I didn't just destroy al-Karak, I destroyed employment throughout the country. After the Bread Revolution, you heard—far and wide—only of unemployed people.

Many of my countrymen who'd also fled to Jordan noticed that, ever since I arrived, the glut of Iraqi refugees was no longer being given visas for the neighbouring countries. Except for Libya and Yemen. For me, Jordan had become unbearable and depressing. I was ready to flee not just to Africa but even to a different planet. The main thing was to get as far away from Jordan as possible. Here, I'd destroyed almost everything.

I LEFT JORDAN AND ITS RUINS and fled to Africa. To be precise, to Libya. Barely had I set foot in the country when—afraid I would devastate everything again—I put my hand on my heart. At first, everything seemed to be in order. One month, two, three, the country was okay—

until it was hit by an almighty hammer. America and other Western governments were demanding more, and stronger, measures against Libya. An embargo. All at once, the Libyan dinar fell to a third of its value against the dollar. From one day to the next, everything became expensive. I told myself that wasn't so bad. But then, news of AIDS suddenly spread round the country. There was talk of doctors and nurses from Bulgaria who had worked in Benghazi and allegedly infected a great number of people, including children, with HIV. This was a scandal among the population. Though no one had exact information about the what, how, who and why of the whole matter.

The next scandal was already on its way. I was still in Benghazi when strange things began to happen in the not-very-distant town of al-Bayda. The Libyan ruler, it was reported on TV, had broken a leg attempting some sporting activity or other. Suddenly only soldiers and policemen could be seen in the streets. Every day, planes flew over Benghazi in the direction of al-Bayda. For days, a deathly hush and fear, both in the town and the eyes of its people. Later, it was rumoured that some people from al-Bayda had tried to kill the Libyan ruler but had only managed to injure him. The town was declared a prohibited area. Rumours spread everywhere that there were nothing but corpses and ruins now in al-Bayda.

If I'd remained there any longer, perhaps the whole country would've been declared a prohibited area.

I LEFT DEATH AND LIBYA and travelled by ship to Turkey. Seven days at sea, hoping for a new beginning, as far away as possible from the Orient. At three in the morning, the captain spoke into his radio: 'We are now entering Turkish waters.'

Five minutes later, he spoke again: 'May I please have your attention!'

A few moments of silence.

'The most powerful earthquake in Turkish history has rocked the country. Towns destroyed, thousands of people killed. More earthquakes are expected.'

Bewildered, I put my head in my hands. 'What have I done?'

The next day, we reached Izmir. Everything looked completely normal—the houses, the people. No sign of an earthquake. I tried to get hold of an Arabic or English newspaper but couldn't find one. That same day, I continued by bus to Istanbul, past many a house that was no longer a house but just a ruin. The journey took quite a long time. Frantic, I tried to sleep in order not to have to look at all the destruction round me.

On the surface, Istanbul was still in good condition, but—upon closer inspection—I spotted, here and there, quite a few destroyed houses. And families camping outdoors, in parks and green spaces. A few were dotted with little cookers and I could sense the chaotic atmosphere in the town. At Otogar, the main bus terminal, I found an Arabic newspaper with the following news:

'At about 3 a.m., in the Marmara region in northwest Turkey, the towns of Adapazari, Gölcük, Izmir and Yalova were rocked by an earthquake, measured at 7.4 on the Richter scale. It is estimated that over forty thousand people were killed and about three hundred thousand rendered homeless.'

I felt an unspeakable grief and feared that my unlucky raven could visit worse things upon the country. The tremors had not yet ceased. Several aftershocks followed that same day but, fortunately, didn't have such grave consequences.

On my first day, I stayed at a hotel on Taksim Square. At midnight, the glass on the bedside table began to tremble. The light bulb hanging from the ceiling, even the bed, were shaking. Invisible hands were beating both the hotel and the earth. I heard shouting. I packed my bag and raced down to the street. The whole wall had a crack down the middle. I decided to sleep with a few others in the park. Admittedly, this disaster had advantages for me. Though I didn't want that, it was in fact the case. I was given free food by various relief organizations and didn't have to pay a single lira for nights in a hotel—for me, a dream, as I had hardly any money. And so, things were relatively good for all refugees at this time in Turkey. No police inquiries. No arbitrary measures to annoy you. No trickery. The police had enough other problems.

For a short time, the earthquake lost sight of Turkey. Then, about three months later, a new tremor took another six and a half thousand lives in the district of Düzce. I could no longer stand being in this country. Whenever I saw a house in ruins or sad, desperate people, I thought it was all my fault.

IT WAS MONTHS BEFORE THE TURKS WERE FREE OF ME and my curse. I reached Athens. Looking about, though, I thought I was in the wrong place. Philosophers, my arse! Nothing but homeless people and refugees. Many of the buildings were destroyed—as if one of the Iraqi wars had passed through. But there was no war. The reason again was an earthquake, the very one that had gone on to devastate Turkey. So Athens was already destroyed when I arrived—a special welcome, probably, personally tailored for me. And to top it all, the hotels were completely full. You had to fight for a space even under one of the many bridges.

Some enterprising people were already making a profit from this situation by selling places to sleep, in parks or under bridges, to people in need. For me, once again, there were only advantages—free food from church-related social groups and, in the end, even a house to sleep in. It's true that, initially, like many others, I slept in many different places, beneath bridges, in the park, in the ruins. But then I decided with a few other refugees to occupy a house. After the earthquake, many Greek families had left their apartments and fled to relatives in the countryside. Others had been evacuated from their homes for safety reasons. Those homes were then locked up by municipal wardens and given a red police seal. We hammered a hole in the wall of such a house in Megalos Alexandros Street and set up home. True, it was pretty much destroyed and without electricity, but at least it had a toilet and a kitchen. We were caught several times by the police and thrown out. We went back each time.

I STAYED IN ATHENS for only a short time and then went on to Patras. That place was teeming with refugees hoping to slip into one of the countless lorries, and thus to board a ship to Italy, illegally. Again, the bringer of bad luck was at my side. It was in the evening. I was lying in the park with a large group of other refugees, from a different Asian and African countries, looking longingly at the ships and the sea and dreaming of the day when I too would manage a trip across the ocean. Suddenly, one of the ships went up in flames. The fire brigade, police and press arrived immediately. There was talk of twenty dead, all Iraqi Kurds. They had hidden themselves in several lorries when the fire—caused, allegedly, by a cigarette—broke out. The next day, the police chased all the refugees from the harbour area. No one was allowed anywhere near the wall. The Kurds organized a demonstration. Demanded proper funerals for the dead. The municipal authorities conceded to the demand. A few days later, we were walking behind the coffins. At the cemetery, one of the refugees turned to me and smiled sadly. 'Look at this dead man! He is my friend. We are from the same village. Now, he has finally found peace and, what's more, a beautiful black suit. He never had one like that when he was alive.'

I didn't answer but walked away in a bad mood and thought, 'All this, only my fault!'

It became difficult to leave Patras and get to Italy. It was months before I managed. I still wonder how—in such a tragic situation—you can apologize enough. For I need to ask a whole lot of people for forgiveness. But I'd rather not think about it. It's fate, isn't it? Or isn't it?

I GOT TO ITALY, this time bringing neither earthquakes nor scandals with me. Thanks to the Italian police who couldn't be bothered to check every one, I was able—quite comfortably—to jump, in Bari, across the harbour fence and to end up, finally, in Bolzano, just before the border between Italy and Austria. At the railway station, a crowd of other refugees had already settled for the night. I managed to get a place to sleep beside a photo booth. People told me that by train or lorry the route to Germany was fast and easy. I was pleased. But that same evening, a people-smuggler turned up with unpleasant news: 'There's no way through any more. The snow's blocked many roads and the police are out all over Austria and Germany. We need to wait for a few days.' These few days became almost a month that I spent cursing myself: 'You jinx, you unlucky raven!' At least I didn't have to apologize to the locals—it wasn't they who were affected by the bad luck.

I ARRIVED IN GERMANY. The inconvenience wasn't so tragic. No big problems. Only small ones. The Germans had jettisoned the Deutschmark and talked themselves into the euro. Everything became expensive. A new immigration act was passed that didn't make life any easier for asylum seekers and refugees. The political Right and Left formed a coalition such that, in the end, you no longer knew what was now Right and what Left. Nonetheless, the feeling didn't ever creep up on me that I was to blame for anything in this country.

I stayed. I started university. Then things took a dramatic turn, after all. Suddenly, some politician or other had the idea of boosting the government's coffers with money from the purses and wallets of the students —and the universities began to ask for up to five hundred euros per semester by way of fees. I decided to apologize to my fellow students.

'I'm sorry!'

'What?'

'That whole fee thing.'

'What about the fees?'

'It's all because of my raven!'

'Raving? Have you gone completely mad or what?'

'No, I mean a different kind of rav-en!'

'Which then?'

'A raven that, at some point, will devastate the earth.'

'You must be mad. What do you mean?'

'Well, you know, the unlucky raven that reached Germany not so long ago.'

'Is this one of your Arabian fairy tales again?'

'Yes, it's a real Arabian tale. Arabian Night Number 1002.'

EIGHT

Return of the Faces

The Iraqis or, to be precise, the Babylonians invented astronomy. They even built the first telescope. Alongside, another kind of science of the stars was developed—astrology. Then, as now, reading the stars is one of the favourite occupations of the inhabitants of the two-river country. The women in my family also proved to be in no way averse to this science. Many ordinary people saw the stars as more than mere shining dots in the firmament. They attributed to them an ability to determine fates. Accordingly, there are stars that signify bad or good days. In mediaeval Baghdad, a system was developed whereby the stars were differentiated and ordered very exactly. This complicated system (of which my mother, too, had total command) included the following fact—there are people whose entire lives are brightly lit by the stars. They are blessed with power and success. And there are people whose lives proceed completely in the shadows of the stars, regardless of whatever efforts they make. They are battered by fate all their lives.

Modern Iraqi history seems to proceed in the shadow of the stars. In truth, though, it isn't led by the stars of astrology but by very different ones. The stars on the epaulettes of the generals, those military monsters who have placed one unlucky raven after another on the roofs of those battered by fate. My life, too, was ruined by these stars in my homeland where I experienced nothing but wars, rebellions and other disasters. These, in the end, sent me off on a long, almost unbearable journey. I changed towns in Asia, Africa and Europe the way other people change their shirts, and tried to put down new roots in every new country and every new town. Again and again, though, the day arrived—or rather, the star—that forced me, usually, for the oddest of reasons, to flee once more.

But what does all that mean? All the wars, rebellions, disasters—and inhuman exertions required by an escape? The stars-on-epaulettes fates that determined my life? Are they just individual incidents in an exciting, never-ending story—to put behind you, like a childhood illness? Or does something else remain deep within, something indescribable and mysterious? A cemetery full of memories of a whole host of nightmares and of dead people? Yes, precisely such a cemetery turned my life too into a hell—the cemetery the stars pre-arranged for me.

I always wanted to free myself of this cemetery but, again and again, faces rose from it that made a suffering Christ of me—or perhaps, to put it more pathetically, and as I first wrote many years ago: 'Jesus went to Heaven but I'm still hanging on the cross.' Again and again, the faces. And not only in my dreams. The faces of relatives and friends who perished in the war, who lost their lives in jail or on the run. Endless corpses—more than there are hairs on my head! I tried, several times, to talk to a psychiatrist about it. That led each time, though, to a packet of tablets—to help me sleep better. But when I asked the doctor about the faces that always spoke to me in the streets, I got no reply or, at best, a childlike, naive one that, even days later, had me and all my faces laughing.

These faces didn't just take me to the edge of madness. They also took my life to the limits of tolerability. They appeared one after another, in different constellations, as if they'd discussed things in advance. Each of these groups tried to trigger memories I'd have preferred to leave to eternal sleep. Recently, the faces of Fadhel and Aga surfaced, surrounded by a number of other faces, in a deep, never-ending stretch of water.

Fadhel was an Iraqi, a good friend I had met in Benghazi. He'd studied English and was especially interested in mythology. His greatest wish was to go to Australia and write his master's thesis on the Tower of Babel. But during his illegal boat journey to the world's fifth and smallest continent, he was seized by the immense vastness of the ocean and swallowed up. In contrast, Aga was an ordinary boy who had the very small dream of sleeping in Denmark, or Sweden, with a great big blonde. He was Iraqi or Persian or neither, he didn't know. During the Iraq–Iran war, when he was still a child, his family was deported to Iran because the Iraqi government regarded them as Persian, and thus as racially impure Iraqis, and treated them as such, though they'd been based in Iraq since the nineteenth century. In Iran, however, it was the reverse—they were seen as Iraqis, not pure Persians, in racial terms. There was only one way out of this dilemma. And so, I met Aga in Turkey when he was trying, with me and some other refugees, to enter Greece illegally. But the powerful deluge of water that was the Ebrus washed him away. Might he finally have found a homeland at the bottom of the river? His and Fadhel's face often visited me, whispering, 'Life is like water, you can't grab it and hold it in your hand. You can only plunge into the middle of it.'

Alla's face often dropped by, too. In his wake, a string of others. I knew Alla from Jordan. A member of a Shi'ite party, he fled from Iraq because the party had been banned there. Abroad, he wanted nothing more to do with politics. He simply wanted peace and quiet, to live in peace. He then tried to go from Jordan to France, illegally. Everything he'd worked hard for in Jordan, about nine thousand dollars, he gave to a people-smuggler for a French passport. Arrested at the airport, he spent a short time in jail and was due to be deported to Iraq. One night, they found him in his cell—dead. He'd banged his head on the wall until he collapsed. Alla's face said to me, 'Life is like a wall. You have to bang your head on it to understand what the truth is.'

Faces and more faces—faces that died in jail, faces that died in the war. Faces that went missing. Faces that became slaves to madness. The face of Mustafa. He, too, fled from Iraq to Libya. In Tripoli, he worked as a chemistry teacher. Then one day he simply went mad. He imagined he was being followed by the Iraqi secret service, that he would soon be killed. He began doubting all his friends and made their lives hell. 'You traitor! You spy! You're working for the secret service.' One day, he even beat up his superior, the director of the Institute for Technology, because he was convinced the latter was an agent of the Iraqi government and was spying on him. He's been in a mental home since. A few years ago, his face appeared before me. I knew right away he'd died. His face, too, was accompanied by a string of others. He didn't say a single word, only looked at me as if I were a ghost. I don't know why. Perhaps he'd told me what he wanted to say and I just hadn't understood.

The face of Zahir came to me too. Oh, Zahir! We first met in Berlin. He was already an old man, almost sixty but looked eighty. He'd left Iraq with his wife in 1979 when the government abolished the Communist Party and persecuted and murdered its members. Zahir then lived in East Berlin and moved to the western part of the city when the Wall came down. Somehow, he didn't ever live in the present. The past had its arms firmly round him. When we met in an Arabian cafe in Kreuzberg, he talked only about the Iraq of the seventies. 'We did that' and 'back then was' and 'those were the best years, after all'. He had no idea of the present, nor did he want to. He talked to me about the communist values that would save Iraq. At first, I wanted to enlighten him, to tell him about the current position in Iraq of the former Communist Party—how only a few old men and women remained whom almost no one knew after all these years. Then I decided to let him revel in his dreams.

Zahir's wife once told me that his suitcase was packed and waiting in his bedroom since 1979, ready for their imminent return to Iraq. He regularly checked the contents to ensure everything he needed was in it. When the war began in 2003, he phoned me, full of joy. 'I'll soon be flying to Iraq!' On 9 April, the big statue of Saddam on Firdos Square came down. That same day, I called him at home. At the other end of the line, his wife's voice: 'Zahir waited his whole life for this moment. He didn't get to experience it. He died yesterday. Heart attack!' Zahir's face had a word of comfort for me. 'The most beautiful paths are those that don't reach their goal.'

Some time ago, the faces of Salim and Hasne—whom I'd almost forgotten—visited me. Salim's face consoled me, 'In war, we are all just lost feathers.' Hasne's face added, 'We mothers are grief's jewellery and its lipstick.' I can now remember Hasne and Salim. It was in the first days of the Iraq–Iran war. I was still a child. One day, some members of the Ba'ath Party, some policemen and a few from the security service, brought Salim into the playground of our primary school. They shot him in front of all the students because he'd refused to go and fight at the front. 'See, children!' our head teacher declared, 'That's what happens to traitors and cowards.' Salim had just turned twenty and was a peace-loving, sociable young man. He was the only son of Hasne, the blind woman, who sat all day at the window of her home, selling sunflower seeds, chewing gum and Pepsi-Cola to the children. Despite being blind, she could easily feel and recognize coins. Following her son's execution, she descended into an abysmal sadness. A month later, she too died.

IN THE SUMMER OF 2006, new faces assailed me. Faces determined to take me away with them. None of the previous faces had tried to do that. The new ones tried all the harder, the faces of Karima, Saber, Basem and Sumeia. They're so embroiled in my fate, they swim in my blood. God, that's a long, long story! Where to begin? It's best if I begin with the fortune-teller.

I'd just turned seventeen when I visited a fortune-teller with my brother Mohammed, two years my junior, and Galil, the boy next door. For the first, and last, time in my life, I wanted a fortune-teller to predict my future. First, Mohammed and Galil heard their futures from the mouth of that old man who was barely four feet tall. He predicted a splendid and successful career for both, as engineers. Then he turned to me. 'Do you really want to?'

'Yes, why not?'

'But, my son! Believe in God—not in fortune-telling!'

I thought he was joking. 'But I want you to!'

He waited a while, looked to his left and right and then said softly, 'Listen. This is your fate. You won't ever have peace. You'll go to jail. Then you'll flee—far away. You'll always be on the run. You'll see the walls of many jails on this earth. You'll travel and travel. You'll live far away, in another country. You'll marry and have a child. Then you'll leave your family and go away. You'll travel some more. You're a hard-working person, my son, but that won't help you because your star in the sky doesn't shine. So you'll always remain a loser. In the end, when you're thirty-five, you'll live in the street with down-and-outs and then die alone in a foreign country on a bleak platform. That is your fate.'

Nowadays, Mohammed is a successful electrical engineer in Baghdad. Galil too. And I? At first, I wasted no time thinking about these predictions. But the first time I landed in jail, I remembered the old man and his words. Meanwhile, I've reached the year of my death. To quote my brother Mohammed, 'You haven't too long to go!' My problem with his prediction is that everything he predicted has actually come true. Everything, that is, except the child. But who knows that for sure. Maybe, there's a woman somewhere who hasn't told me everything . . .

Actually, I've always wanted a child. But I was also always scared that it would kill me. Yes, I have to admit, I *am* afraid of dying soon. I always imagine sitting at home, in the year of my death, with the windows and doors barricaded, doing nothing special. I do have one tiny piece of hope, though—the fortune-teller forgot something important. The faces in my life. And that includes the new ones. He didn't know everything after all, even if he made out that he did. My new story is also the story of the faces that go with my fate.

IT BEGAN WHEN I WASN'T EVEN TWENTY. In 1991, after the Second Gulf War, a new chapter in Iraqi history began—Shi'ites in the south and Kurds in the north took to the streets, protesting against the government. This kindled resistance that spread like wildfire. Many Iraqi towns fell into the hands of the opposition. Only Baghdad and a few other places remained—places that belonged to the family or, rather, *tribe* of the dictator. In Baghdad, everyone was waiting for the Kurds from the north and the Shi'ites from the south to come marching. Rumours were circulating that they were already on their way. They were taking their time, though. Too long. And so the people in Baghdad, especially the Shi'ites from our part of town, al-Thawra, and from the district of al-Shala, tried to put up resistance like the Shi'ites in the south and the Kurds in the north. All they reaped in return, though, was death, grief and poverty.

A short time later, Iraqi troops attacked the country, turning the towns in the north and in the south into sad landscapes—nothing but ruins. The whole world watched as if the Iraqis were chickens that could be butchered without any sense of guilt or morals getting in the way. Corpses, everywhere you looked in the streets. Mourning in every destroyed home. And why? This interrogative particle was enough to make my youth go to hell. Why? And again, why? At school, I ended up in circles that collaborated with secret and banned parties, communists, religious people and patriots. They talked about being betrayed by the tolerant world powers who had allowed Saddam to crush the uprising using rockets and bombs. Actually, it wasn't hard to understand that Ba'ath Party and its leader Saddam were the ravens that brought ill luck to the Iraqis.

Since the appearance of Saddam, the new president, everything in Baghdad had changed. The bazaar, just a few metres from our house, was practically empty in the days in which the former president had been removed. Pictures and photos of the new president were suddenly all over the district—the president with a big moustache and in uniform; the president wearing a turban and a dishdasha; the president with a cigarette; the president with his daughter; the president with builders; the president with a group of embarrassingly clean schoolchildren. My father, too, dragged home a huge portrait with a golden frame in which the great dictator could be seen sitting, holding a sword, also golden.

'What's that?' my mother asked.

'Shut up,' my father snapped. 'Just hang it up. I don't want to hear a word!'

The same portrait was hung by the head teacher above the entrance of Sinai Primary School for Boys and

Girls, so that all those who entered could see it. In every classroom, too, a picture was put up above the blackboard. In it, the president, dressed in a milk-coloured dishdasha, a red-and-white spotted scarf and a turban on his head, smiled paternally.

Through the streets walked the demon that stole little children. Though no one could see her, everyone knew she was there. Everyone stared at her from the windows, especially the mothers. Prayers and incense flowed through the streets as if we were entering a new life in which everything was to be questioned. My mother was in no doubt that the demon could come up through sinks or taps. Which was why, in those days, she always carried the Koran with her. Even to the toilet. She put any number of amulets round the house. Above the television in the guest room, she put a hand made of plaster, decorated with tiny pieces of green glass and painted eyes and Koranic verses. A green sandal, also made of plaster, decorated the wall above the front door so that anyone who approached the house would be shooed away. Above the door to the guest room on the other side of the yard, she fixed a black–blue metal eye. Back then, incense was lit at least four times a day and the Koran read frequently. My sisters Karima and Farah sat with my mother every evening, reciting the 'Throne Verse' countless times: 'Allah! There is no God but He, the Living, the Eternal! No slumber can seize Him, nor sleep. All things in Heaven and Earth are His. Who could intercede in His presence without His permission? He knows what appears in front of and behind His creatures. Nor can they encompass any knowledge of Him except what He wills. His throne extends over the heavens and the Earth, and He feels no fatigue in guarding and preserving them, for He is the Highest and Most Exalted.'

I was given a new amulet too, to go with the old one I'd been wearing round my neck since my childhood. The new one, like the old one, was woven from green material. I don't know what the muezzin had written on it, nor where I lost both on the same day.

The local boys left home in the morning, wearing khaki-coloured clothes. Sometimes, they carried weapons or drove past in khaki-coloured cars. Men with big moustaches and white, hard, rosy-cheeked faces—the likes of whom the residents had never seen—drove by. They always stood around outside the school, then went away with my father or other men from the local Ba'ath Party whom I didn't know. They sat for hours in a classroom in the Sinai School that had been placed at their disposal as an office, before driving off in their beautiful, new white cars. My father and his friends waved after them, endless joy in their eyes.

Odd things began to occur. Many policemen patrolled the streets at night and it was rumoured that a few boys from the neighbouring districts had suddenly disappeared. Other strange stories were told too. My mother, though, feared only the demon.

'She now has children!'

'Who?'

'The demon!'

'If it was only the demon we had to worry about, everything would be fine!' my sister Karima sighed.

Unknown men filled our district. They carried pistols and rifles. Everything had changed. After that or, to be precise, after the execution of Hasne's son, Salim, another curse fell over the town. The fallen—many of them—returned from the front in coffins. My brothers had to join the army too, like many young men in the neighbourhood. My father—like all the old men—had to go to the People's Army. The members of the People's Army were really funny. They wore striped uniforms, carried old weapons and you could always hear their hoarse little coughs before their fat bellies came round the corner. My father had sentry duty once a week. It made him feel especially important, as if he was holding up the state singlehanded. My mother, on the other hand, with the advent of war, became a very sad creature. She followed the battles on TV. In no time at all, she knew by heart all the names of the army corps at all parts of the front, especially those where my brothers were stationed. On Friday afternoons, she shared her knowledge with other women and discussed the course of the war. When the first funeral procession passed, though, she slapped her face, screamed and descended for a few days into something illness-like. The first funeral procession was followed by many others, all decorated with the national flag. A new coffin—daily. It's no exaggeration to say that the name Baghdad was no longer appropriate. Better would have been Madinat al-Jetheth—city of corpses.

I REALLY DID HAVE PLENTY OF REASONS to label the members of the Ba'ath Party ravens that brought ill fortune. But that helped no one, not me either. For two years I worked with banned parties. I wasn't a member of any but I did help where and when I could. Distributed posters, secret letters, forged documents. Tried to persuade the young men round us to join. I was motivated, above all, by rage. But a little by my naivety too. I hadn't the slightest clue what I was risking. Just knew I wanted to work against these ravens. I often think, nowadays, about this stupidity that changed my life. But every time I also think that if history ever repeats itself, I'll still do the same.

Two years later, in March, I heard that the police had arrested Qasim. He was a joiner and worked in a Shi'ite party. I knew him very well. Yes, I'd already even worked for him. We'd been in the same class for a year at grammar school. I once distributed a flyer for him with the slogan 'Liberation is our goal'. After a few months, Qasim was executed. I was now afraid but no longer afraid that he'd told the authorities about me. Moreover, I never had the feeling I could end up in jail. Throughout, I tried not to think of what had happened to Qasim and I stopped meeting the younger men.

At the same time, our large family had a new addition. Saber—the child of my sister Karima and my friend Sadiq. Karima was a teacher and Sadiq a lecturer in literature at the University of Baghdad. They were, so to speak, my actual family. I spent most of my spare time with them. Sadiq was a great friend of mine. Together, we read works banned by the government and listened to music declared sinful. Three months after Saber was born, I found myself in jail.

Qasim had, indeed, not betrayed me. It was another prisoner, who knew Qasim, me and many others, who had given them a lot of names. As a result, at the end of November that year, the police rounded up forty-one people. The boy who'd revealed our names worked as a police spy for a year before finally—as I later learnt—fleeing to Iran. After Saddam was overthrown, I discovered the guy again on Iraqi TV. In the media there, he was celebrated as a fighter and politician. In Iran, and now also in Iraq, he'd managed to end up in important political positions. His face is on Iraqi TV every day. His mugshot on the billboards in the streets.

IN JAIL, there were neither heavenly nor earthly paths. Only walls, hunger, lice, torture and instruments of torture, rats, prisoners, ghosts, guards, police magistrates, dampness, skin diseases, fear, struggles for survival . . . Many of my friends died while being tortured or of hunger, and their sad faces accompany me to this day. I, though, somehow survived. It took a long time but at some point I was released.

The day after my release, Karima said to me, 'The child's face didn't radiate positively in our lives.'

'Why do you say that?'

'He sent you into jail. He must have been born under a bad star.'

'That's superstition. Don't talk nonsense!'

I felt a bit strange, though. Of course, it couldn't be Saber bring me bad luck. At the time, I was less interested in superstitious fate stuff, more in how I could get far away from Iraq as fast as possible. Despite that, the words of the fortune-teller haunted me—he had predicted I would leave Iraq. It seemed he had been right.

Shortly before I fled Iraq, Karima became pregnant again with her second son, Basem. Two months after he was born, I found out I could go to Jordan. My sister laughed on the phone: 'Basem's got a good kick! He sent you far away! He was born under a good star!'

'You're mad!' I replied. She laughed and laughed, could hardly stop.

But my escape to Jordan was actually an escape into a second hell. Those Iraqis who could flee to Western states at least found security for life and limb. In other Arab countries, such as Jordan, life was hardly any different from that at home under Saddam. Not only because almost the same kind of dictatorship existed there but also because many Arab peoples thought Saddam a hero. A symbol of the cohesion of the Arab nations and their power. They therefore viewed the exiled Iraqis, especially the opposition members, as traitors. Iraqi exiles consequently lived in misery and fear, also of their fellow countrymen. For, in the neighbouring states at that time, countless spies and members of the Iraqi secret service were up to tricks.

I remember, in Jordan in the nineties, an unwritten law existed whereby an Iraqi could be deported to his homeland if a Jordanian accused him of a crime. For that reason, many Iraqi opposition members, who had continued to be politically active in exile, suddenly disappeared. Completely apolitical people—who only wanted to live in peace—were suddenly no longer about.

Where else could you flee? Back then, only a few countries remained to which a mere mortal of Iraqi background could travel. Not a single Western state would give an Iraqi a visa. Plus, to get to the West, illegally, cost around ten thousand dollars. Where was I to get that kind of money? So I went to Libya.

IN LIBYA, I lived like a down-and-out, had some work every now and again, a place to sleep every now and again. After I'd been in that sandy, dismal country for about a year, Karima came to Libya with her family. They too were fed up with Iraq. They too were trying to make a new start. They found an apartment in Misde, a little town in the desert. At the arse-end of the world.

For me, exile was somewhat more bearable. Though I was working in various other towns, between five hundred and a thousand kilometres away from Misde sometimes, I went to visit them twice a month and spent the time with the children. Karima cooked her best dishes, specially for me, and told me news she'd gathered from her women friends. I loved the way she told stories, the kind of passion she had. As she sat at home all day every day, looking after the children and, thus, not leading a very varied life, she was a master in making every banality sound exciting and important. I call this ability 'the imagination of Arabian housewives'.

Sadiq, lecturing in literature at the teacher-training college in Misde, could be depended on for the most recent books. With him, I could always discuss the most interesting topics, about which not everyone in this dull sea of Arabian sand could, or would, speak. My nephew Basem was very like me. He always said he wanted to be a poet like his uncle. He was soon known to, and popular with, all the Iraqis who lived in the neighbourhood. He had an incredible talent for mimicking people and bestowed us with many relaxed and cheerful hours, in which—for a short while—we could forget the misery round us. Saber, on the other hand, was more like his father. Calmer, more serious, more of an intellectual. At school, he always had the best marks and sometimes asked questions that I could understand and answer only after some serious thought. Karima's family was my oasis in the Sahara, a substitute homeland.

Three years later, I learnt that Karima was pregnant again. 'Let's see where you end up this time!' Sadiq joked.

'Not Africa, I hope!'

'But we're there already!'

For me, it already didn't matter. I was living in the middle of the desert—what else could possibly happen! The third child was a girl—Sumeia. 'At last, a girl!' We were all pleased. Three months after she was born, I was forced to leave Africa and head towards Europe, alone. My passport was due to expire soon. And living in the desert without a valid passport wasn't a good idea.

AT THE END OF MY LONG JOURNEY, I landed in Germany, in Munich. Karima wrote, 'Our Sumeia has a good kick too. You're in Germany. Finally, you've found a good star. You can now find peace of mind. Sumeia deserves a German gift from you!' I wrote back, 'No more children, please. The fourth will probably send me to my grave. And your new star will soon receive her German gift.'

Many years passed. Iraq was ravaged by war again, Saddam's dictatorial regime was destroyed and a new government created under the American occupation. Karima and her family returned to Iraq. Once again, they were dreaming of a new beginning. Karima got a job as a school inspector, Sadiq as a lecturer at the university. Still, they were unable to find peace of mind. Another new form of war was waiting for them. The old followers of the Ba'ath Party, Arab nationalists, the neighbouring Arab dictatorships, Islamic groups, the Iranians, the Turks, various Iraqi ethnic groups, the Americans and their allies and many others turned the streets of Baghdad, and a number of other Iraqi towns, into a blazing hell of bombings and street battles. Iraq was like a stadium in which every single team wanted to win the game. And so, once again, countless corpses in every corner and every hole of the country struck by disaster.

'The stars don't want to change,' was Karima's commentary on the situation facing Iraq. Sadiq was considering going into exile again. Instead, he reached for the phone. 'Your sister's pregnant again!'

'What?'

'It was a mistake. We've had a row and she's with her family.'

'How come? Why the row?'

'I don't want this child. What am I supposed to do with it, in this chaos?'

'No idea! And what's Karima saying?'

'She wants it.'

'I'll speak to her and see what she says.'

Karima wanted the child and Sadiq was forced to accept it. In Germany, though, I was trembling and thinking, 'Where will this child send me?' The boy was born—Ayad. His kick wasn't so hard. He only sent me from Munich to Berlin. Munich University was again demanding a load of paperwork, as is customary in Bavaria.

Berlin, on the other hand, offered me uncomplicated admission to the Studienkolleg, a compulsory preparatory course for foreigners wishing to study. And so I went to Berlin for a year.

I NEVER RETURNED TO A PLACE. I always travelled on, and always when one of Karima's children had given me a good kick. This time, though, I returned to Munich to finally begin studying properly. But who could have anticipated what a tragic blow my return would trigger!

At the end of August, the news reached me through the Arabian online press: 'Karima Hamid, sister of Iraqi writer Rasul Hamid, wife of Iraqi literary critic Sadiq Hasan, and three of her children, Saber, Basem and Sumeia, have been killed in a terrorist attack in Baghdad. The survivors, her husband and her youngest child Ayad, were seriously injured.'

On the phone, I couldn't find out much. 'Bomb outside the house' and 'Who?' and 'Why?' No one had any details. The police said, with a shrug, 'unknown terrorist organization'. I've lived through countless terrible times but this was too much. I couldn't, and wouldn't, believe it. When their faces visited me for the first time, though, I knew they were no longer alive. Their faces—pale, sad, like all suffering faces—are now my constant companions. They don't say much. Just that they miss me. Karima's face, though, set me in a new dilemma, 'We have changed fate and the stars.'

'How?'

'Simple. Saber is fifteen, Basem twelve and Sumeia eight. That makes thirty-five.'

'And what does that mean?'

'That's the thirty-five years the fortune-teller predicted for you.'

'I don't understand!'

'You don't have to.'

Karima would say no more. She'd just look at me, like the others. Since these new faces have begun coming to me, I've changed my opinion about dying. I'm no longer afraid. When death does come, I'll open all my windows and doors and prepare to embrace it as I would a lover. I'll be able to join the new faces and go to my eternal rest. I'm no longer afraid of the year in which I'll die. I'm even looking forward to it. It will be the first time in my life when I won't lose and I won't cry. Instead, I'll be lost and people will cry for me. And the faces will no longer haunt me and drive me to madness. Maybe, I'll be a face myself and visit someone else.

If I've understood Karima correctly, though, I won't have to die at thirty-five. That said, I'd like to reach a special goal and ask all the stars to allow me the time to do that. I want to—finally—finish writing my story. From the faces—via the miracles—to the birth. Or vice versa. The dedication has already been decided:

> *For those who, a second before they die,*
> *still dream of two wings.*

18.14. The childlike smile of my girlfriend, Sophie, awaits me on the platform in Munich. Her eyes light up when she sees me. She waves at me. It's good to see her again, after the disturbing journey. A warm embrace, and we get straight into her car.

Should I tell her what happened? The whole thing with the manuscript, I mean. But what should I say? That I found a manuscript containing my story? Written by someone also called Rasul Hamid? And with no address or phone number on the envelope? Should I tell her I met a ghost called Rasul? That's more, surely, than plain 'unrealistic'. It's ridiculous, even. 'Will you go and see a psychiatrist, please!' I can hear it already—the categorical imperative.

Finally, after supper, I excuse myself. Say I need some time on my own. I'm incredibly tired . . .

I lie down on the couch and think about what I've experienced. A terrible nightmare. What sense am I supposed to make of all this? How could someone have written my story, put it in an envelope and then left it right next to—of all people—me? If someone stole my story, why did he make sure it got to me, of all people? And the many details that no one could know but me? How did he get hold of them? Even the handwriting is like mine, down to the last dot. Very tiny. Illegible, almost. And in pencil. He changed only a few names, the details of a few incidents. But that isn't significant. It remains my story, only mine. And then the idea, the structure. My style, exactly. How did he manage to steal that? From my head? I hadn't discussed it with anyone. So a lot of people knew of my plan to write my life story. But no one knew the exact approach—not even me, until recently. I'd thought about it for a long time. Again and again, I tried to find a form that would allow readers to begin wherever they liked. Each chapter would be a beginning and an ending. Self-contained, yet an essential part of the whole. A novel, a short story, a biography, a fairy tale—all brought together in one work . . . That had been my—and only my—idea, damn it! And now, one of the many demons in my life had turned up, wanting to take it all from me. My life, my idea, even my soul?

For a long time, I'd been meaning to commit my odyssey, my journey on the ghost ship, to paper. I'd never managed. Time and again—in the past five years, at least—I'd tried to start. And time and again I stopped because I wasn't convinced, because I didn't have the right structure, because I simply wasn't satisfied. I always knew exactly *what* I wanted to write; only never *how* to. Almost a year ago, I'd finally had the crucial idea but didn't have the time to act on it. So, really, I should be glad someone else did it for me! What counts, when it comes down to it, is: I'm now holding my story in written form. Or is that *not* what counts? All I want to do is sleep . . .

The sun is shining in. Sophie kisses me, whispers in my ear, 'Wake up, *Habibi*, the weather's wonderful outside! Don't forget, you wanted to send your book off today. Get up!'

I look out of the window at the trees, the foliage, I can hear the birds. Idyllic, almost.

'Really, what a lovely day!' I get up, shower, head to the university. First, I attend a lecture, then I go to the computer room, to read the news. At lunchtime, it's the Café an der Uni. A recently acquired habit I enjoy—sitting in a cafe, reading, writing or watching people.

Empty. Totally empty. The feeling, for a moment, I'm all alone, in the city. That the people have vanished were never there at all. Empty. And all bright and clean. No students any more, no cars or buses, no fountain on the square, no main university building. Nothing—only me and a wide, empty Ludwigstrasse, the vast nothingness round me. Where, in fact, am I? What am I doing here? Where's everyone else? Questions like these boom in my head—like drums at an African festival. Empty, like a never-ending desert, bare mountains or clear water. Eerie too, like a forest after a violent storm. And my questions, loud, yet quiet; echoing, though unvoiced.

After a while, I come back to my senses. Once again, I was, mentally, completely disoriented. But, thank God, as I look along Ludwigstrasse—this time, there are no African drums—everything has returned: the old university building, the cars, the students . . .

I look round again, paying more attention now. Girls and boys, ladies and gentlemen—constantly on the move, now it's summer. Appreciating the ambience, they stroll along Ludwigstrasse, then Leopoldstrasse, until they reach Münchner Freiheit. Hardly a seat to be had, outside the cafes. Pigeons and sparrows, wherever you look. Some have even made their nests in the roofs of the majestic buildings that line this splendid avenue. A male bird is seducing a female. The male spreads his feathers, drags them along behind him, then swaggers round the female, flirting. 'Coo, coo. Coo, coo.' The female, head held high, struts up and down before him like a queen. She moves, at times slowly, at times quickly, driving the male wild. Not far from the male, a student is chatting up a girl, or trying to. The girl smiles. Bravely, he swaggers round her. She makes straight for the entrance to the underground and he follows, blindly. 'Jonas, wait for me!'—a second student, waving madly, shouts across the street.

I ENTER THE CAFE and take a seat at a free table. Put the rucksack between my feet. Place a notebook, a book, a packet of cigarettes and a lighter on the table. Light a cigarette . . .

14.16. I open my rucksack and put an empty envelope on the table. A few people leave, others come in. A woman and her two children, adolescents, sit at the table next to mine. They're not saying a word.

Headphones on, the girl is listening to music on her MP3 player. The boy sits in the seat beside her and turns on his laptop. The woman has her mobile phone to her ear. Finally, the waitress appears. She's young. Eighteen to twenty, say. Her hair is dyed red and she's wearing jeans and a white T-shirt, 'Sexy Girl' printed on it. Small, firm breasts support the lettering. I order a large coffee and a glass of tap water.

14.45. I open my rucksack, remove the manuscript, put it in an empty envelope. And seal it.